MW00913280

REVENGE

BY THE ARNO

ALSO BY ANN REAVIS

Italian Food Rules

Italian Life Rules

Cats of Italy

Murder at Mountain Vista

The Case of the Pilfered Pills

Death at the Duomo

Secret of La Specola

Tim,
It's time to experience
Italy for awhile
Thanks
Ann

REVENGE

BY THE ARNO

A Caterina Falcone Mystery

By
Ann Reavis

REVENGE BY THE ARNO

This is a work of fiction. Names, characters, organizations, places, events, and incidents are either products of the author's imagination or are used fictitiously. All events at or descriptions of actual locations in Florence, Italy (government buildings, museums, restaurants, and/or stores) are used fictitiously. Any resemblance to actual persons, living or dead, or actual events is purely coincidental.

Copyright © 2018 Ann J. Reavis
All rights reserved.

ISBN-13: 978-1790346844

Published by Caldera Books
Email: calderabooks@gmail.com

Cover by Kelly Crimi
Interior book design by Bob Houston eBook Formatting

Without limiting the rights under copyright reserved above, no part of this publication may be reproduced, stored in, or introduced into a retrieval system, or transmitted, in any form, or by any means (electronic, mechanical, photocopying, recording, or otherwise) without the prior written permission of the copyright holder of the book.

First Edition (December 31, 2018)

For their passionate love of Florence and the Florentines this book is dedicated to Joe and RoJean.

CHAPTER ONE

Channeling her personal Jane Austen, Caterina Falcone thought that it was a truth universally acknowledged that any phone conversation in Italy would be, at least in part, about a meal already consumed or one to be enjoyed in the future.

With a cell phone wedged between ear and shoulder, Caterina buttoned a crisp cotton blouse, while discussing the family Sunday lunch, three days hence. The only oddity about the call was that it was with her mother (born and bred in Boston), not her Florentine father. She interrupted to ask why.

"Your father had to go to the market at the crack of dawn. Gianluca is coming in from San Miniato with white truffles, the first of the season," Margaret Mary Gifford explained, before adding, "And even though they are more expensive than gold, Gianluca will sell those fragrant nuggets before the morning is out, or so says your father. He's determine to be serving them at Osteria da Guido at lunch today."

Picking up her cup of cooling cappuccino from the kitchen counter, Caterina took a sip. "I may have to reconsider my pizza date tonight and instead take Rafe to dinner at the Osteria. White truffles shaved on hot buttered *tagliatelle* is not to be missed." She left her cup in the sink and went in search of a jacket.

Her mother's voice sharpened, "We certainly are not going to serve truffles for the family's Sunday lunch; Lorenzo's children need something simpler…"

The phone slipped from Caterina's shoulder, bounced off the leather sofa and slid under the coffee table. She swore as she scrambled after it. She heard, "…you still there? What do you think?"

"Think about what?"

Her mother's tone iced over, "About guinea hen with seasonal vegetables. Really, Caterina, I know you have to go to work, but we could get done with this in a couple of minutes if you would just pay attention."

"*Faraona con verdure arrosto* is a perfect choice, mother. But you know that Babbo is going to change the menu while he's at the *Mercato Centrale* this morning. He'll see a pork loin or maybe a fish so fresh he can't pass it up." She stepped into a pair of loafers.

"I know. I know," Margaret Mary admitted. "I used to think it was a good idea that he decided to close the

Osteria on Sundays and cook a family meal at home. But now I'm not so sure."

Peering out of the long narrow window set high in the back wall of her living room – Caterina's apartment, once belonging to her paternal grandmother, looked over the terracotta rooftops of Florence's Oltrarno neighborhood – she checked the sky for rainclouds, before observing, "Think about me living next door to the two of you. Now I'm commandeered into being his Sunday *sous-chef*." Caterina's parents occupied the apartment across the landing. Their place had a terrace that overlooked the Arno River.

Her phone started to vibrate. She looked at the screen and told her mother, "I'm sorry. I have to take another call coming in."

"I surmise it is the tall American whose mother named him Raffaello? Am I wrong or is he your dinner date tonight?"

"I'll call you later," Caterina said as she tapped the screen of her phone and brought it back to her ear.

"Rafe?" It was Rafe Mathews, the tall American. Her mother was prescient, as ever. "I'm still at home and late for work. Can I call you in an…"

He interrupted, "Good. I'm glad you're on this side of the river. You need to get down here now."

"Down where?" She put the cell phone on speaker mode, setting it on the coffee table.

"Just upstream from the Vespucci Bridge on your side of the Arno. You know, near the spillway in the river."

"Why?" She slipped one arm into a jacket that matched her charcoal gray wool slacks.

"There's a black guy and an angry mob – if four guys can be a mob – and there may be a body in the weeds."

She couldn't have heard correctly. While shrugging the jacket on, she picked up the phone, flicking it off speaker as she put it to her ear. "A what?"

"A body. I was taking my morning run along the Arno and heard these guys yelling," Rafe Mathews explained. "I'm going down to see what I can do to stop them, but you know my Italian is abysmal. So please hurry."

"Stop them from what?"

"Killing the guy." Rafe cut the connection.

Caterina grabbed a raincoat and her purse, before racing down six flights of stairs to the front entrance of the riverside apartment building. In an adjacent alley, she stuck a key into the seat compartment of her Vespa, pulled out the helmet and replaced it with her purse. She simultaneously took her seat, pushed the scooter off its kickstand and revved the engine. It took her only two minutes to zoom down Lungarno Guicciardini to the location Rafe had described, just east of Ponte Amerigo Vespucci. She bumped the Vespa on to the sidewalk, out of traffic, parked it, and removed her helmet as she looked over the retaining wall to the the narrow strip of mud, dirt, and tangled grass along the river.

Rafe, dressed in shorts and a black tee shirt, was standing astride the sprawled body of a man whose espresso-colored skin and drenched clothes were streaked with mud and blood. In front of Rafe were four men, two with clenched fists, one carrying a shovel, and the last nursing a bloodied nose.

Caterina yelled in Florentine dialect, "I'm calling the police." She pulled her cell phone out of the pocket of her coat.

The four looked up. Rafe kept his stance. The Italians were all shorter than the American, but were well-muscled, dressed in clothes worn by construction workers or day laborers.

She waved her phone at them before calling 113, the emergency police number. She identified herself and requested to be rerouted to the San Frediano *Commissariato di Pubblica Sicurezza*, the precinct office for the San Frediano neighborhood, the closest to her location. She told the receiving officer that there was a crime in progress and requested an immediate response. As she started down the nearby stone stairway to the river, she heard a siren's pulsating wail just a few blocks away.

She stopped before reaching the bottom step, seeing for the first time the trouser-clad legs of a body lying face down about fifty feet upriver from where Rafe stood over the unconscious man. The body was partially hidden by the tall grass that grew down to the water. One arm trailed in the current of the Arno.

CHAPTER TWO

Turning to the most immediate problem, Caterina yelled again at the three men advancing on Rafe; the fourth man hung back nursing his bloodied nose. "*Polizia*! Back up. Against the wall." She pointed at the brick retaining wall.

"Lady, stay out of this," said the oldest worker, whose weathered skin looked as tough as the worn leather jacket he wore over a jumpsuit streaked with paint. "We were just trying to stop that *pezzo di merda* from throwing a woman in the river. He was getting rid of his victim." His guttural dialect betrayed his familial origins from somewhere near Lucca.

"*É vero*! *Giusto*!" The other men grumbled in agreement.

Caterina held up a hand. "You can either address me as *Ispettore* Falcone or you can shut your mouths until they get down here," she snapped back, realizing too late that her warrant card was in her purse in the compartment of her Vespa, but pointing at two uniformed police officers leaning over the wall of the street above.

The laborers ignored her, watching as the two *poliziotti* descended the stairs while unsnapping the leather guards on the holsters containing their sidearms. One approached Rafe and the other marched toward Caterina and the workmen.

She held her arms out to the side, hands visible and open, while saying in a rush, "I am *Ispettore* Falcone. I'm the one who called in the alert. I work out of the Questura on Magistrate Paolo Benigni's staff." She gestured behind her back, not taking her eyes off the young officer, whose nametag over his breast pocket said "Conti" and whose hand was still on the grip of his gun. "These men must be detained. They were observed assaulting the man on the ground."

Caterina saw Officer Conti's partner draw his weapon and wave it at Rafe, while yelling, "You! Hands in sight! Move over to the wall! Down on your knees!" Rafe put his arms up and then clasped his hands behind his head. He did as directed although Caterina knew he didn't understand one word that was being said. The gesture with the gun was clear enough.

"Officer Conti, please tell your colleague to holster his weapon. That man is known to me. His name is Rafe Mathews. He's just an American tourist — a friend of mine — who happened to witness these four men beating that poor man. Rafe was just trying to keep them from killing him."

Conti seemed to ignore her. "Serroni, keep him on the ground," he told his partner. "At least until I figure out what's going on." He turned back, looking past Caterina. "You four, go stand against the wall."

"But, officer, he broke my nose," complained the injured man.

Another added, waving his arms, "Officer, we were the ones trying to help that girl."

"*Silenzio*! You'll get your chance to talk soon enough." He turned to Caterina. "Let's see some identification."

"My warrant card is up in my Vespa," she said, pointing up to the street. "Officer Conti…"

He interrupted, "Go get it."

"But first…"

"Am I not making myself clear? Either get your identification or get up against the wall with the others."

She walked over to the bottom of the stairs and turned. "You might want to see if he's still breathing. An ambulance would probably be useful."

Officer Conti swore and pulled out his phone.

Caterina was half way up the stone stairway when she stopped again. "And there's another body up in the weeds." She pointed. "She is presumably the woman these gentlemen are talking about."

Officer Conti flipped open his phone again. This time she could hear him calling for reinforcements, including his commanding officer.

When Caterina descended the stairs, Conti was upriver on the muddy path. He leaned over the body and pressed two fingers against the neck. "It's a woman. She's dead."

Even though she had assumed the truth of the matter, Caterina caught her breath at the finality of the statement.

Officer Serroni was leaning over the barefoot black man who appeared to have regained consciousness. Caterina showed him her police identification. He nodded and waved her over to where Rafe was sitting. "We'll get to you in a moment, *Ispettore*."

"How long is this going to take?" yelled the old house painter. "We have work to get to."

"As long as it needs to," snapped Serroni. "Shut up."

Caterina leaned against the wall next to where Rafe sat. "Are you okay?" The pungent odor of the river mud and silt left from the last time when the Arno spilled over its banks almost made her tell him to stand up and stay dry, but she didn't want to antagonize the officers.

"Yeah, they didn't try to take me on." He looked up, his gray eyes sparkling with humor.

"The police or the fine citizens over there?"

"Either. One punch to the face of the biggest one was all it took."

She noticed his sweat-stained t-shirt clinging to his lean torso. "Are you going to get a chill? Do you need...?"

His chuckle cut her off. "You know us Americans. We're tough, not like you delicate Italians."

She gave his shoulder a swat. "Did you tell the police that you are on leave from the FBI, Mr. Tough Guy? Sort of a brothers-in-arms friendly chat?"

"Hard to do when I don't have much of the lingo and I bet they don't understand English. And…"

She interrupted, laughing. "You have enough Italian. '*Sono* Rafe Mathews, *Americano* FBI.' Pretty simple." She wanted to reach out and brush the wavy lock of hair off his forehead, away from his eyes. Instead, she crossed her arms, looking back at the body in the weeds. A chill wind blew her curly auburn hair this way and that, into a tangle.

"And, as I was about to say, they don't seem too interested in who I am or my opinions."

"So what do you think happened here?" She buttoned her coat, wishing she had grabbed a scarf on the way out of the apartment.

"The way I see it, the black guy sees a body in the river or maybe even someone struggling against the current."

"How do you know that?"

Rafe pointed up the river near the woman's body. "Notice just before the weeds start? There's a pair of shoes. He takes his shoes off so they don't get wet or weigh him down in the water. He goes in the river – see he's all wet – and pulls her out."

"Where do our concerned citizens come in?" She glanced over to where Officer Conti was talking to the laborers.

"They are on their way to work and see him trying to resuscitate her. They think he's assaulting her and rush down to save the white woman from the black man."

She instinctively recoiled from the thought. "Why does race have anything to do with it?"

"They would have stopped to ask what happened if he had been white-skinned European or even, American. Instead they just started punching him. He was on the ground when I got down here. He wasn't going anywhere. They were kicking him. His nose is broken and maybe his jaw." He paused, leaned forward and narrowed his eyes, as if to see the injured man better. "But maybe not, because he's able to talk."

"To you?"

"No," Rafe said, holding up a hand as if to tell her not to talk. "He's saying something to that cop who waved a gun at me." He listened for a few more seconds. "I think you're going to be needed."

She refocused on Rafe's face. "As a witness to your complaint for police brutality?"

He laughed, shaking his head. "He was just doing his job. I take no offense. I meant you are going to be needed in an official capacity."

She disagreed. "Not my job, Rafe. Now that they are here, I can go on to work as soon as they get my statement." She could hear the approaching sirens of both police and ambulance.

"First of all, you're going to have to translate for me while I give my statement. That's in your job description, right? Helping tourists who get in trouble with the law."

She nodded, seeing his point. "It must have slipped my mind." She made a big thing about looking for her cell phone. "I'll call the magistrate and tell him I'm on the clock. Duty calls."

Rafe ignored her joking tone. "Second, I think the guy on the ground speaks only French. Officer Serroni can't seem to communicate with him. That is also your job, supporting foreign victims in police matters, right?"

Caterina focused on the man on the ground, trying to hear what he was mumbling. Serroni had clearly given up trying to talk to him, standing to one side, staring at his cell phone screen. She swore under her breath.

"Right?" Rafe repeated.

"Wish it weren't so," said Caterina, pushing off the wall. She walked over to where the man, who she was starting to assume was from Ivory Coast or Senegal, was still prone, one eye open, the other swelling shut.

"Do you understand French?" she asked in that language.

Serroni whipped around, startled at her proximity, protesting, "*Merda*! Get away from him." Caterina ignored the officer, concentrating on hearing any response.

The man nodded.

She squatted beside his head. "Do you speak Italian?" she asked in French.

He shook his head.

"Do you understand Italian."

He answered in French, "A little."

Caterina stood. "Serroni, I told Conti over there that I was a member of Magistrate Benigni's staff at the Questura. You may or may not know that the magistrate runs *la Task Force per gli stranieri*. We are charged with investigating certain cases where foreigners are the victims or perpetrators of crimes in Florence. I'm guessing that's the situation here."

Serroni sneered. "And I'm guessing Benigni's department doesn't deal with illegal immigrants. This African scum is no tourist."

Her tone hardened, as she stepped into his personal space, sticking a finger out at his chest. "That remains to be seen since you can't understand a word he says. Mr. Mathews, over by the wall, *is* an American, speaks no Italian, *was* threatened by that gang, and *may* have to defend against a spurious charge of assault. So this *is* going to be a case assigned to me, no matter what." She heard pulsating sirens approaching so she added, "My guess is that I will be making the acquaintance of the captain of your precinct in a couple of minutes, so maybe you will want to keep your racist opinions to yourself."

"*Capitano* Ventroni won't..."

Caterina interrupted, "I'll just step out of the way while you bring him up to speed, but I'll be listening in case, as I suspect, this is going to be *my* case, not yours, by the end of the day."

CHAPTER THREE

Magistrate Paolo Benigni sat back, manicured fingers steepled against his lips, listening closely as Caterina briefed him. When she had finished he commented, "I certainly expect that the fate of Adamou Nadja is going to be your number one priority next week. The mayor has already called me."

From the other side of the antique desk, Caterina looked up from her notes. "The mayor? Why?"

"He is getting a lot of resistance to his liberal immigration policy. Any good story about an undocumented refugee behaving heroically is welcome news at the Palazzo Vecchio." The magistrate checked his watch. "It's almost lunchtime. When did the doctors at *Ospedale di Careggi* say you could visit Mr. Nadja?"

"Since he didn't need to be taken to surgery for his broken ribs or nose, he was admitted to the general medicine ward. They're worried he may have a concussion, but Dr. Monterosso said I could come by this evening."

"Before then, can you write up a briefing report for the mayor? Just a sketch of where our hero is from and perhaps how he got to Florence."

Caterina frowned and shifted in her chair. "I don't know much about him except he's from Niger, not Senegal or Ivory Coast as I had assumed. It makes sense since Niger is hemorrhaging refugees after the last drought. I looked up the latest U.N. report. Did you know that the average birth rate in Niger is almost eight children per family?"

"You know I leave those esoteric details to you, but it is exactly what the mayor is looking for." Benigni ran a finger down the page in front of him. "How old did you say the young man is?"

"Twenty-four. But I haven't confirmed that information. He had a document from the refugee center in Bari in his jacket pocket. That's how I got the little information I have, like name, age, country of origin, and the fact that he entered Italy three months ago."

"How did he get here? Has he been in Bari all of this time?"

"I'll get that information this evening, I hope." Caterina closed her notebook. "A bigger problem is the dead woman whom Mr. Nadja pulled out of the Arno. We still haven't identified her. We don't know if she is

Italian, a foreign resident or a tourist. We won't even know how she was killed until the coroner examines her later this afternoon. She did have a cell phone in her pocket. If they can dry it out, perhaps we will have a lead."

"I may have a clue." The magistrate's other investigator Marco Capponi spoke from the doorway.

Caterina turned to see that, as always, Marco was impeccably dressed in a fine woolen suit, jacket buttoned, with a light blue tie, cinched tight. The magistrate waved him in, pointing at the second carved wooden visitor chair in front of his desk. Unlike most offices in the Questura, the magistrate had personally furnished his suite, including the adjacent reception area, with his own antiques, carpets and art.

"What do you have for us, Marco?"

Capponi placed a piece of printer paper face down on the desk, unbuttoned his jacket, sat down, eased his trouser leg, and shot his cuffs before he spoke. The magistrate gave Caterina a wink and crossed his hands on his chest as he leaned back in his chair, waiting. It was the only hint Caterina had that their boss thought Marco was as officious as she did.

"I was scanning the reports of the various precincts as I do every day at noon and then again at six before I leave for the day," Marco explained. He paused and looked up at the magistrate. Caterina wondered if he was waiting for a pat on the head.

"And?" The magistrate's smile tightened.

Marco placed a page on the edge of the desk in front of him and paraphrased as he read, "The Palazzo Pitti station reports that two officers on patrol on the *Ponte*

Santa Trinita stopped a tourist from Australia as he climbed off of the large triangular space atop the pylon on the northwest end of the bridge." Marco stopped reading, to add, "You know where they've spent hundreds of euro to put up those ugly metal railings to stop people from crawling out to take selfies, but really the railings only help the tourists get a good handhold to lower themselves over the edge." Seeing both the magistrate and Caterina nod, he continued, "It was just getting light at eight. They showed him the sign that said sitting on that part of the bridge is illegal."

"What does this have to do with the body in the river?" The magistrate's impatience was evident. Caterina thought he was probably late for a luncheon appointment.

"The police were suspicious because he was shouldering a backpack. They thought he had spent the night on the bridge, sleeping rough."

The magistrate got up, took his jacket off a hook on the wooden stand behind his chair, and put it on. "Marco, I still don't understand why you made the connection to Caterina's case."

Marco cleared his throat. "The Australian had a purse."

The magistrate stopped. "A purse?"

"What kind of purse?" asked Caterina.

Marco read from the report, "A woman's large blue and green leather purse or satchel. Clearly not his own." He looked up and summarized the rest as the magistrate sat back down in his chair. "It seems that as the two *poliziotti* were crossing the bridge they saw this man shove the purse into his backpack. With reasonable suspicion that he was a thief, they searched his pack and retrieved the woman's bag."

"I assume the gentleman – do we have his name? – has been detained at the Palazzo Pitti station."

"Yes, sir. They took him into custody on charges of trespass and suspicion of robbery or burglary." Marco ran a finger down the report. "His name is Donald Mundt." Marco spelled the last name for the magistrate's benefit.

Caterina, who had been jotting notes throughout Marco's report, asked, "Why do you think the purse belongs to my unidentified victim? Did Mr. Mundt confess to stealing her bag? How did she get into the river?"

"Caterina, if you had been listening, you would remember that I said I had *just* read this report. I do not know *everything*, but the connections seem apparent to me. Donald Mundt told the police he found the bag near where he left his backpack. He claimed that he planned to turn it in to the administrative offices at the Palazzo Vecchio, since that was the only government building he knew of."

Caterina wasn't convinced. "So why did you make the connection?"

"The way I analyze it is that the illegal African tried to steal the purse on the bridge during the night and in the struggle pushed the woman over the edge into the Arno. He then discarded the purse on the pylon near Mundt, while he was sleeping."

"That is *absurd*," said Caterina. "Why would he then run down the Lungarno, dive in the water and pull her out?" She stood up, unable to continue listening to such unsubstantiated drivel.

"Because he didn't want to be charged with murder." Marco emphasized each point with a tap of his silver pen on his leather-bound notepad. "The only way he would have known she was in the water is if he had pushed her in."

"And Mr. Mundt slept through the assault and the theft?"

"I assume you will find that…"

"This is all speculation, you two." Benigni turned to Marco. "Let us back up a bit. Caterina told me that there is evidence that Adamou Nadja was camped beside the river on the Oltrarno side down by the Ponte Amerigo Vespucci. There is also evidence that he was packing up his site this morning at about seven when he saw a body floating in the river. He went in and pulled her out, only to be set upon by some passing construction workers."

"He would say that," Marco opined.

"He hasn't *said* anything, *Marco*." Caterina spit out his name instead of calling him a nitwit. "The evidence at the scene tells me this."

"Are you sure you read it right?" asked Marco, pointing his pen at her.

Caterina brushed aside the question. "Was there any identification found in the purse?"

He scanned the report. "A passport for Alice Perkins, a driver's license with the same name with an address in Camden, Maine, U.S.A. No money beyond some coins." He looked up. "See? I am right. It was a robbery."

Caterina ignored the assertion. "Credit cards? Bancomat card?"

"None. Just a guidebook, a hairbrush, a scarf, and some cosmetics."

The magistrate stood again, sweeping the papers on his desk into the center drawer. "Caterina, if Marco is guessing right and the purse belongs to the drowning victim, then she is an American. For now, since you are following that case on behalf of Mr. Nadja, assume the victim is a foreigner and follow-up with the coroner. The case of this Australian also may fall under the purview of this office, so contact the *Commissariato di Palazzo Pitti* and ask for notes of the interview with him, or, better yet, see if you can sit in on any further interrogation."

Caterina wrote out a list in her notebook, responding, "Yes, sir."

"Maybe they didn't notify the Task Force because Mundt speaks Italian or they chose not to arrest him," said Marco.

Caterina thought he sounded irritated because he wasn't going to be involved in the case. She limited her response to, "We're not a translation service, Marco. They should have sent us an email when they detained Mr. Mundt."

In the work of the Special Task Force, Caterina was usually assigned all cases involving foreigners who spoke English, French and German. Marco got the Spanish-speakers, Eastern Europeans and Russians. Those victims or perpetrators from Asia or the Middle East were split between the two since, to date, they had been rare and the services of a free-lance translator would be employed.

Seeming to sense the discord, the magistrate turned to Marco as he walked toward the door. "How is that case you are working on where the Syrian gentleman was found at the Four Seasons with a stiletto in the back of his neck? Is his family still here? Have you helped them arrange for the transport of his body home?"

Caterina stood, forestalling Marco's response by saying, "If you don't need me for this, sir, I would like to see if *Capitano* Maggio over at the Palazzo Pitti station will let me see Donald Mundt. Maybe Mr. Mundt saw the woman who owned the purse or the woman who ended up in the Arno." Then she extended a tiny olive branch to Marco with a glance. "Perhaps they *are* one in the same."

The magistrate waved her through the door. "Go. Go. After that head up to Careggi Hospital and see if Mr. Nadja can give you any more details. If he is really the hero you think he is, the mayor wants to be informed. I want a briefing before you leave tonight or, at the latest, first thing tomorrow morning."

"I will also try to get a report from the coroner," Caterina said as she slipped past him. "We need to know if the woman in the river was there by accident or intent."

CHAPTER FOUR

At the coffee bar across from the Questura, Caterina ate a *panino* with prosciutto, pecorino cheese and arugula, and followed it with an espresso, before riding her Vespa across the city to the Oltrarno police station of the Palazzo Pitti precinct.

Captain Maggio had agreed on the phone that she could sit in on the second interview of Donald Mundt, the Australian tourist, saying that he would delay the questioning if she could get there by three. Maggio told her that Lieutenant Capra was assigned the case. Caterina knew Leo Capra, having worked with him on the homicide investigation three months earlier in July, when a British student had been murdered in a museum near the Palazzo Pitti.

When she asked Captain Maggio if he was handling the situation of the girl found that morning along the bank of the Arno, he said, "That's being investigated by Gianni Ventroni out of the San Frediano precinct."

Before she left the scene near the Vespucci Bridge that morning, Caterina met Captain Ventroni. He directed her to "get out of the crime scene" because "the *disgraziato nero* is being taken to the hospital so your French is not needed; not that it was any help anyway since how could a black African speaking French make any sense anyway." Caterina hoped that she would not have to consult with Ventroni any further about the dead girl, but she had a sinking feeling that the issue of the assault on Adamou Nadja was going to require her to communicate with the belligerent *capitano* again.

At two forty-five, Caterina asked the young officer behind the counter at the entrance of the Palazzo Pitti station to let Lt. Capra know that she had arrived.

The door opened behind her. "Caterina! I told Captain Maggio that we should just get you a desk here." Leo Capra, muscular, handsome, thirtyish, a couple of years older than Caterina, walked past carrying a small white paper bag. He waved her through the turnstile at the end of the counter and down the hall.

"I just picked up a *pappatacio* for a mid-afternoon snack." He opened the door to his office. "Come in and tell me why you are interested in this kiwi."

"A 'kiwi' is a New Zealander, Mr. Mundt is Australian." She put down her briefcase beside the gray metal visitor chair in front of Leo's small desk that just fit in the tiny office. "The Task Force didn't get notification that you had detained him. Marco Capponi found his name on the mid-day report."

"Of course he did." Lt. Capra shook the pastry to the front of the sack. Using the bag to keep his hand from getting sticky, he took a bite. He chewed and swallowed before responding, "I didn't think it was important to let your group know about this tourist. We're going to release him if he can come up with 160 euro to pay the *multa* for trespassing on the *pigne del ponte*, you know, the four enticing flat platforms over the river at Ponte Santa Trinita. The mayor spent 7,500 euro to put in the barriers to keep idiots on the bridge, so we have to enforce the fine to pay for what has turned out to be metal handrails, not barriers." He took another bite. "Anyway, he speaks enough Italian, so I didn't think we needed to bother you."

"We aren't a translation service, Leo, although sometimes it seems that way. It's true we don't usually get involved with minor infractions, but from what I can tell from the report he had a purse that didn't belong to him."

"Mundt said he found it and it will be hard to prove otherwise unless you have the owner of the purse swearing out a complaint." He finished the raisin-studded pastry, crumpled the bag, threw it in the wastepaper basket, and opened the file in the center of his desk.

Caterina leaned back in the chair. "So why do you still have him here? He was picked up eight hours ago."

"Like I said, Mundt has to come up with 160 euro. And you called my boss and asked to interview him."

Capra ticked the points off with the fingers of his right hand. He got to the third digit and paused, glancing at Caterina. "And I wasn't that comfortable with his explanation about the purse. He was telling me that he 'just happened' to find it on the bridge when Captain Maggio came in with the report from San Frediano that the body of a woman had been found in the river." He stopped and flicked a crumb off his desk. "I decided to let him cool his heels in an interrogation room until I got some facts on the other case. Then you called so I had one of the girls get him some lunch and I told him I would get back to him about now."

"Do you know anything more about the dead woman? I suspect Captain Ventroni isn't going to be in any hurry to send information my way."

Leo grinned. "Making friends as usual, Caterina?"

"Something like that."

Capra tapped the open file. "I haven't been able to get a photo of the deceased to compare with the passport found in the bag." He slid a piece of copy paper across the desk. The facsimile of the U.S. passport showed an unsmiling photograph of a woman with straight highlighted brown hair, pencil-thin plucked brows, and a birthdate that claimed that Alice Perkins was thirty-one. "Ventroni claims this matches his victim, but like I said, he hasn't reciprocated with a photo. I guess you know she had a *telefonino* in her pocket that they are trying to access."

Caterina nodded. "Can I see the driver's license?"

He passed her another page. The photo was similar although the license was issued four years earlier than the passport and Alice was sporting a blonde perm.

"Have you asked Mr. Mundt about her?" Caterina pulled her notebook out of her briefcase and jotted down the address on Harbor Road, Camden, Maine, from the license.

"I decided to wait for you. As you say, anything bigger than a minor infraction, your crew gets involved."

"It would make it shorter if you give me a report of your conversation this morning."

"I'll do better than that. I'll give you the recording. But long story, short…," he said, sorting through the pages in the file to find some scribbled notes, "Donald Anthony Mundt is forty-two and comes from Brisbane, Australia. He claims to be traveling on a break between jobs as an IT specialist at a telecom company. It's one of those treks that those 'down under' specialize in, world travel lasting six months or more."

"How long has he been on the road?"

"He entered Europe three weeks ago through the Frankfurt airport – I already confirmed this – traveled south through Germany and Austria, and came into Italy last Saturday, October 10. He claims to have arrived in Florence yesterday, Wednesday."

"Is he registered at a hotel in town?"

"That leads us to the bridge," Capra said, looking up from his notes. "It seems that he is sleeping rough most nights, getting a bed at a hostel or cheap hotel once a week to get a good night's sleep and a shower."

Caterina tried to comprehend. "Are you saying he slept on the bridge last night."

"So he claims."

"Wasn't he worried about falling off? There aren't any railings on the outside edges of the pylons. Or, at the very least, concerned about getting rousted?" Her voice became teasing as she mused, "Although I guess it's totally possible that the fine officers of the Palazzo Pitti station didn't patrol the bridge in the night." Her pen hovered over the page as she waited for his answer.

Lt. Capra squirmed in his chair. He put his notes back in the folder, closed it and slid it to the side of the desk. "It seems that there was a game of *Scopa* being played in the station common room … and … well, long answer, short … two officers are on a weeklong suspension."

"Okay, so we have reason to believe that Mr. Mundt slept on the *Ponte Santa Trinita*. Did he see any women on the bridge after midnight?"

"I haven't asked him that question or any others. We had just gotten to the explanation about his night when Captain Maggio came in with the note for me about the body in the river."

Caterina slipped her notebook back in her briefcase and stood. "Let's go ask him about Alice Perkins. Bring that file, okay?"

CHAPTER FIVE

Caterina thought Donald Mundt looked too composed for an innocent man who either had been detained for over seven hours for no apparent reason or for a man guilty of the murder of the woman whose purse he stole. She paused in front of the one-way glass window in the wall of the small interrogation room. Mundt appeared to be snoozing or meditating while sitting on a metal chair behind a rectangular table. His brown hair, close shaved on the sides and wavy on top, was just touched with silver, but the two or three days growth of beard showed significantly more gray. Of medium height with a wiry build, wearing a black cotton sweater and black jeans, he would not stand out in a crowd, she thought.

Lt. Capra passed behind her and opened the door. When Mundt opened his eyes to watch their entrance, she noticed they were a light blue. His feet were shod in worn high-topped black sport shoes. The room had a residual odor of the tuna sandwich that the Australian must have been given for lunch.

Leo Capra handed Mundt a small bottle of water and made the introductions. "This will probably go faster if *Ispettore* Falcone asks the questions in English instead of the mixture of Italian and English that Mr. Mundt and I used earlier. As before we are recording this session."

"Anything to wrap this up would be appreciated," said Donald Mundt, his voice low and quiet. "Although I'm just sightseeing, there are still more picturesque parts of your city than this room. And as I said before, although I didn't see the sign prohibiting me from sitting on that part of the bridge, if you would escort me to a Bancomat, I can pull out enough money to pay the fine."

"Good afternoon, Mr. Mundt," Caterina said as she took one of the chairs on the opposite side of the table. "I'll try not to duplicate the questions from this morning, but I'd like to clarify a couple of things."

"Sure," he said, crossing his arms over his chest.

"Lt. Capra told me you entered Italy almost a week ago. Is that correct?"

"It was Saturday and today is Thursday, so yes."

"When did you get to Florence?"

"As I told him, yesterday."

Caterina looked at her notes and then at his face, watching for his response when she asked, "You claim that you did not know that sitting on the pointed platform of the Santa Trinita Bridge was trespassing, but you didn't just sit there, did you? You told Lt. Capra that you slept there last night. You must have realized that was not allowed."

His expression did not change as he reached out to pick up the bottle of water and twist off the cap. "If I had thought about it, I might have guessed that I would be rousted. But I was kind of past thinking. I crawled out there about midnight with a couple of bottles of beer, after drinking a few earlier with a group of Brits on that odd porch with the bronze of the wild boar. You know, the one where the market carts clear out around eight."

"*Il Mercato Nuovo con il Porcellino*," murmured Capra.

Caterina nodded and asked, "Are you saying you were drunk when you got to the bridge?"

Mundt nodded, "And got drunker still while enjoying the view. So I don't really remember making the decision to sleep on the bridge. It just happened."

"Was there anyone else on the bridge when you were there? Did the British drinkers come with you?"

"No, I left them, but there was a guy and a gal on one of those triangular open decks on the bridge. They invited me to join them. They had a bottle of wine and some stuff to eat."

"Were they Florentines or tourists?"

"She was American and the guy was from Ireland." Mundt took a drink from the bottle of water.

"Did you catch the man's name?"

"Ian something."

"And the woman?"

"I think her name was Alice. I don't think she told me her last name. She was pretty deep into that bottle of wine."

Caterina wondered why Mundt didn't know Alice Perkins's full name. When someone finds a purse, the first thing they do is check whose it is, she thought.

She decided to go at it from a slightly different direction. "When the police detained you there was a purse in your backpack. Where did you find it?"

"It was *under* my backpack. When I picked the pack up this morning, I found it."

"Did you check inside the purse to see whose it was?"

"I didn't get a chance. The cops yelled at me to get on to the sidewalk, off the pylon."

Caterina sat back, scanning the small sterile room, not really seeing it, trying to imagine his version of the story. It was plausible, she concluded.

She turned to Leo Capra. "Passport, please." He handed her the photocopy.

"For the recording, I'm identifying this paper as a copy of a page from a passport issued in the United States." Caterina placed it in front of Mundt. "Was Alice Perkins the woman drinking on the bridge?"

He picked up the page, stared at the photo and read through the identifying information. He put it down and looked at Caterina. "It could have been. The name fits. It was dark and I was pretty drunk."

"When did Ian and Alice leave the bridge?"

"I don't know. I went to sleep. When I woke up, he was gone, but she was still there."

"*Cosa?*" Lt. Capra yelled. He turned to Caterina and said in low fast Italian. "He didn't tell me anyone was there when he woke up."

"If I understand you right," said Mundt, "you didn't ask me if anyone was ever with me. You just asked if I knew who owned the purse." He picked up the bottle of water and finished it.

"Let's break this down a bit," said Caterina, taking a deep breath. "Who was on the concrete platform on the northwest end of the Santa Trinita Bridge when you fell asleep?"

"Me, Ian and Alice."

"When did you wake up?"

"About six thirty."

"So it was still dark."

"Yes."

"Was Ian there when you woke up?"

"No."

"Was the woman you knew as Alice there when you woke up?"

"Yes." Mundt looked like he was trying not to laugh at Caterina's staccato questioning.

She kept her eyes on his face, looking for any prevarication or half-truth. "What was she doing?"

"She was asleep, wrapped in a poncho or some sort of big shawl."

"When did she leave?"

"I don't know. She was gone when I got back."

Caterina glanced at Leo Capra, who was glaring at Mundt. Poor Leo, she thought, if you don't ask, you don't get the info. She asked, "Where did you go?"

"I had to take a piss. So I thought I would find an alley or someplace to take care of the problem," he explained, his Australian accent getting broader. "But after I walked a ways, I thought I might need better facilities, if you know what I mean," he said, not looking at Caterina, but meeting Leo Capra's frowning stare. "When I'm sleeping rough, I sometimes use a hotel lobby restroom to clean up."

"Where did you go?" Caterina repeated.

He looked back at her and grinned, as if at his own private joke. "To the Excelsior, just downstream past the next bridge."

"Did you take your backpack?"

Mundt shook his head, becoming more serious. "I've found that if you wear a pack into a hotel lobby, they ask you to leave. If you come in, looking like you've been out for a walk or a run, they usually let you by. Since the woman on the bridge – uh, Alice – was there, I thought my pack was safe and anyway it was shoved up against the wall, not easily seen from the sidewalk."

"How long were you gone?"

"Twenty or thirty minutes, maybe more. I used the toilet and then washed up a bit."

"What did you think when you got back and Alice was gone, but her purse was still there?

"I figured that, like me, she had gone off to find a bathroom."

"And left her purse?"

He shrugged. "I don't know what kind of shape she was in when she woke up. Or maybe she didn't see it because my pack was on it. Or she thought it had fallen in the river."

"Did you wait for her to come back once you found the purse?"

"That's exactly why the cops caught me. I waited. The sun was coming up. She didn't return so I thought I would head out and leave her purse at the Palazzo Vecchio." He pointed at Capra. "Like I told you, Lieutenant. I assumed there would be a lost and found depository there."

Caterina sat and thought for a moment, running back over his answers so far. Time to get to the heart of the matter, she thought. She glanced at Lt. Capra, who nodded.

"There was a woman pulled out of the Arno this morning. Do you know anything about that, Mr. Mundt?"

"*Where*? What part of the river?" He looked quickly back and forth between the two of them. "I certainly did not see anyone swimming in the river. There's a pretty good view, up and down the Arno, from where I was standing. If someone was in the water at around seven thirty, I would have seen them."

Caterina allowed the silence to stretch, waiting for the realization to come to him.

"You mean it was *her*? This Alice person? Is she okay? Why was she in the river?"

"That is what we are trying to determine, Mr. Mundt. The woman in the river is dead. We still don't know how she died. We also don't know if she is Alice Perkins, the owner of the purse found in your backpack."

"You don't think I had something to do with this?" Mundt pushed back his chair. "I tell you she was sleeping when I left and she was gone when I came back. I know nothing about the woman you found. I have no reason to wish anyone ill or to lie to you."

"But you already lied to us. You didn't tell the officers on the bridge or Lt. Capra here that you knew who owned the purse. You didn't mention to Lt. Capra that you spent the night of the bridge or that there was a woman named Alice with you."

"I was just trying to keep it simple. I didn't lie. No one asked me any questions about how long I was there or about anyone else. It's not a lie. It just didn't come up."

"That may be, but you do see how your lack of candor complicates the situation, don't you?"

"Look, I don't know what's going to happen next here, but I've told you what I know." He looked back and forth between the two officers.

CHAPTER SIX

Visiting hours at Careggi Hospital had already begun when Caterina arrived to interview Adamou Nadja. She waited for the elevator while arranging where and when to meet Rafe Mathews for pizza and beer.

"I can get anywhere in town in about an hour or maybe a bit more," she said softly into her cell phone so as not to disturb those clustered around the elevator.

"How about nine," he said. "I'm at my apartment near Piazza Tasso, so where do you want to go?"

"We can probably get into 'O Munaciello on Via Maffia. It's close to you and I have my Vespa. Can you call and make a reservation?"

"Hey, aren't you the Florentine? Why don't you call?"

"It's good practice for you and I'm just getting into an elevator at the hospital."

"As good a *non sequitur* as I've ever heard."

The door slid open and out walked ten or so people, including Magistrate Paolo Benigni.

"Gotta go," said Caterina. "See you at nine at the pizzeria." She ended the call.

Apparently her boss, dressed in the same tweed jacket and dark olive slacks he had been wearing at the office, hadn't seen her so Caterina followed him out the exit door.

"Sir," she called. "Magistrate Benigni."

He turned and his eyes seemed to clear as if clouds of deep thought passed. "Caterina, what are you…? Oh yes, the young man. I forgot you were scheduled to interview him this evening."

"But, sir, what are you doing here? Did you want to talk to Mr. Nadja, as well? Actually, it makes sense. Your French is as good as mine, probably better."

He gave her a small smile, but shook his head. "It's my mother. She was admitted this afternoon to the cardiac unit."

"I'm so sorry to hear that, sir. I hope it's not serious." She stopped, thinking that was a stupid thing to say. "I mean. of course it's serious, if they admitted her, but I …"

He put his hand on her arm. "I understand what you are saying, Caterina. It is something we have anticipated and should have taken more seriously when she was a decade younger. She needs a stent in one of her cardiac arteries. The only problem is her age. She is healthy, but turned ninety-one this past May."

"When are they doing the procedure?"

"Tomorrow morning."

"Is there anything I can do?"

"I've notified Patricia. She'll take care of my calendar." Patricia Benvenuti was the magistrate's administrative assistant.

"I'll let Marco know not to expect to see you until Monday and I've got my to-do list. There's nothing that can't wait for your input."

"Nevertheless, I believe if all goes as well as expected tomorrow, I will be in to get briefings from both of you in the afternoon around one. So be ready to update me on your interview with the gentleman here and the … where is he from? … oh yes, Australia … the Australian from the bridge with the purse. And the coroner…"

Caterina broke in. "Sir, sorry to interrupt, but really we'll handle things. I have my assignments. Marco has his. Don't worry about anything. Just your mother. I'll be in the office all morning, but don't worry if you can't make it."

The magistrate scrubbed a hand over his face. "Thank you, Caterina, I know I can count on you." He turned and strode off down the walkway to the parking lot.

Caterina was still thinking of the magistrate's mother when she walked off the elevator on the third floor, the inpatient unit for general medicine patients. She asked the nurse at the central staff desk where Adamou Nadja was located, and was directed to the last room in the south wing.

The room contained two beds with a curtain between them. The bed near the door was empty. The room smelled of rubbing alcohol and pine cleaner. As she walked past the curtain she found the refugee from Niger in the bed by the window. He was staring out through his one open eye at the rosy dusk that was fading in the hills protecting the city below.

"Monsieur Nadja, you may not remember me from this morning," Caterina started in French and then introduced herself.

As he turned from the window, she could see that his right eye was completely swollen shut and the other was blood red around a tiny black pupil. His nose was taped and his nostrils stuffed with cotton gauze. He breathed through his mouth. His bottom lip was split and covered with ointment.

Through the thin hospital gown she could see his ribs were wrapped tight with white tape. A sheet was pulled up to his waist. From an IV pole a bag of clear liquid hung, dripping into a tube that ran to a tiny needle inserted just above his left wrist. Two of the fingers of his left hand were splinted and taped together. She hoped, but didn't have much faith, that the men who were responsible for his condition were in jail.

"I remember." His voice was raspy.

She saw a small open plastic bottle of water with a straw out of his reach on the bedside table.

"Would you like a drink of water?"

He nodded. She brought the bottle to him. He took it in his uninjured right hand and with a bit of help from her was able to get the straw to his lips. He drank between breaths until there was only an inch of water at the bottom of the bottle.

"I'll get you another before I go," she said, pulling a small over-the-bed-table into place.

He lay back, seemingly exhausted from the exertion.

"Can I ask you a few questions?"

He nodded.

"I know it's hard to talk when you can't breath through your nose, so just nod or shake your head," she instructed. "I understand you are twenty-four years old and from Niger."

He nodded.

She sat in a chair beside the bed and pulled out her notebook and a pencil. "What town were you born in and were you living there before you left the country?"

He took a big breath. "I was born in Bilma where my family are farmers. We had a small orchard of date trees."

His voice was clearer and stronger, but he seemed to have a lisp. She wondered if he had lost a tooth in the assault.

He took a breath. "I learned French at school and since I was the second oldest boy, I was sent to the Madama outpost in the north." Breath. "To work for the French troops stationed there. The money was better and my parents had plenty of children to pick and dry dates."

"Why aren't you still in Madama?"

"It went well for about three years, but six months ago there was a car that exploded at the entry to the camp. It was set by Boko Haram." He took another sip of water. "The French colonel in charge was killed. The replacement officer didn't like me and sent me home."

"Why are you in Italy? Why didn't you go back to Bilma?"

"I am over twenty and not married. The harvest failed. My father said I must find work in France. I traveled through Libya to the coast and came to Lampedusa in a boat overloaded with migrants three months ago."

"Were you in the refugee camp on Lampedusa?"

He shook his head against the pillow. "They sent me to Bari. I was in the detention camp there for two months. I tried to get a temporary visa to get to France, but it was denied. Since I was not under threat of death in Niger, your government wants me to go back."

It was a common story to Caterina. Asylum seekers might get the rare visa. Economic refugees rarely did. "How did you get to Florence?"

"First, I tried to get into France without papers."

"How did that work?"

He took a deep breath. "I got a ride on a long haul truck full of tomatoes. It was going to Genoa. Then I took the train to Sanremo." Breath. "I then walked and took buses to the border. I walked across on the railroad tracks, but got stopped in Menton just on the French side of the border." He stopped talking and looked out the the window at the dying light. "Since I didn't have papers, the police drove me back to Sanremo and dropped me off with a bunch of other Africans. The Sanremo police are brutal, so I decided to come here with a couple of men from Burkina Faso."

"Had you met them before?"

"No, but one of them said there was work selling things to tourists in Pisa and Florence and that I could make some money. He knew who to contact once we got to town. It's easier to hide in a big city than one of the small towns on the coast." He paused and met her eyes. "And it is starting to get cold."

"So you've been in Florence for a couple of weeks?"

He nodded.

"Did you get a job selling things in the street."

"I bought a box of selfie sticks and resold them to tourists. Then I was given some of those wire necklaces, the ones with English names twisted in the wire, on consignment. They were harder to sell. One day I had posters, but the police grabbed those."

"But they didn't arrest you?"

"I ran."

Caterina moved to a new subject. "Did you make an application for a visa here?"

"Yes, but I have been told by other applicants like me that only about two percent of the requests from countries like Niger or the Ivory Coast are granted. Italy thinks we are the responsibility of France, our old colonial masters." He closed his left eye.

"I know you are tired, but we must talk about what happened this morning." Caterina turned the page in her notebook. "Tell me the story starting with last evening. How did you end up at the Arno?"

"For the last couple of nights I have been sleeping at an encampment under *Ponte all'Indiano*, but there was a Congolese guy who was making a mess, yelling and fighting. I decided to move last night, so I could get some sleep." He finished the water in the bottle. "I'd noticed an unlit stretch of the embankment that was dry between the Vespucci Bridge and the Carraia Bridge. Above that spillway."

"What time did you get there?"

"A couple of hours after the midnight bells."

"What happened then?"

He smiled as best he could with a split lip. "I slept. Really well."

"When did you wake up?"

"I don't know. It was still dark."

"The sun comes up around seven thirty this time of year."

He frowned and was silent for a moment. "It was coming up when I saw the woman in the river."

Caterina felt a chill go down her back. "Was she swimming, struggling, floating, what?"

"She was already dead. I saw drowned bodies in the Niger River once. Boko Haram then, too." He stopped, then took three quick breaths through pursed lips. "She was floating face down in a calm area out of the current; just bumping against the wall upstream from where I slept."

"What did you do?"

"I took off my shoes and went in after her."

"So she was beyond the point where the dirt embankment ended." Caterina sketched a map in her notebook of the area as she remembered it.

"She was about two meters upstream from where the dirt and weeds end. The water comes up to the wall there."

"How did she end up so far downstream? I mean, after you got her on the shore. Why didn't you just pull her up into the weeds at the tip of the embankment?"

"I misjudged the speed and depth of the river. The bottom drops out fast there, so I was swimming when I got to her. The current caught us and I thought we were going over the spillway, but then my feet touched the bottom and I got her on the bank. I was trying to turn her over when those men came running up. I thought they were going to help, but they were yelling and then they were kicking and punching me." He was panting, his eyes squeezed shut.

She didn't know if he was just out of breath or in distress. She waited a full minute and as he became calm, she said, "They claimed that they thought you were assaulting the woman."

He opened his left eye. If anything, it looked redder than before. "That makes no sense," he said, his voice high and tight. "They must have seen me in the water. It takes time to get down to the river from the street. They attacked me without asking anything. I did not even have time to roll her over or to pull her further from the water." He stopped to breathe and asked, "Do you know who she is? I asked the police and the doctors, but they would not say. Or maybe my Italian is just too bad to understand."

Caterina assumed that all of the police he dealt with were of Captain Ventroni's ilk. They weren't going to give Adamou Nadja an iota of courtesy, she thought, even though he had acted heroically.

"We are trying to determine that right now. I think we will have an answer tomorrow morning."

To herself, she promised that if the San Frediano station didn't send a photo of the victim to her tomorrow that she would go to the coroner's office and take it herself.

"I will come to tell you what I learn tomorrow evening," she told him.

"That would be very kind of you."

She stood, putting her notebook in her pocket. "Now I'm going to let you rest, but don't be surprised if someone from the mayor's office turns up tomorrow."

"The mayor?"

"You are going to be treated as the hero you are, I believe."

"I hope not," he whispered. "I have been trying to be invisible."

"Adamou, call me unrealistically optimistic, but I always believe that good acts reap rewards in the long run. I think your life is going to take a turn for the better. Or at least it will after your nose and ribs heal."

Fifteen minutes later, she was at her Vespa, putting on her helmet when her phone rang.

"*Pronto,*" she answered. "*Pronto?*"

"*Ispettore* Falcone?"

"*Si dimmi.*"

"It is Oscar at the coroner's office. Dr. DiPiero asked me to give you a call. Your name is on the file for the woman pulled out of the Arno."

"Yes?"

"He told me to tell you that her blood alcohol level was point two zero percent. She was very intoxicated."

"Was she dead when she entered the water?"

"Dr. DiPiero hasn't finished the autopsy. His report should be typed up tomorrow morning, but he wanted you to know that she was very drunk when she died. I guess you called in with that one question this afternoon."

"Yes, I did. Thank you for getting back to me tonight. Oscar, could you do me another favor?"

"Of course. That is, if I'm able."

"I need a good photograph of her face. We are trying to get an identification. Could you take a couple for me?"

"Of course. They will come with the report, but if you give me your email, I can send a couple to you in the next hour."

CHAPTER SEVEN

Rafe locked eyes with Caterina under the giant papier-mâché angel flying across the vaulted red brick ceiling. "Would you go to a wedding with me?"

Caterina choked on the sip of wine she had just taken. "Say what?" she sputtered, dabbing her lips with a napkin.

Pizzeria 'O Munaciello was full and it was hard to hear each other as the sound of many languages echoed off the stone walls. Caterina wasn't sure she heard him right. A spicy aroma of tomato, garlic, oregano, and basil wafted up from his half-eaten sausage pizza and her *pizza Margherita*. They had just finished discussing her interview with Adamou Nadja and the growing problem of undocumented refugees in Italy arriving on the ever-increasing armada of boats from Libya.

"Did you say 'wedding'?" She reached for a piece of warm bread from the small paper bag in the center of the table. "I was just talking about you getting frisked this morning and your mind moves to weddings?"

He bit the tip off his last piece of pizza. "Actually they didn't frisk me – an oversight on their part, but of course I wasn't wearing much, just shorts and a shirt."

"I suppose you FBI guys are all 'my hands are registered as deadly weapons' or something like that," she said, making air quotes with her fingers.

He looked at her over the rim of his beer mug and murmured "Not just my hands, ma'am." He swallowed and added, "I've never thought that Italy brewed up good beer, but this is definitely pizza-worthy."

"Don't change the subject," she retorted. "What wedding?"

"It's not exactly a ceremony. That wouldn't be allowed here. It's more of a delayed wedding reception. Really just a big party."

"What do you mean? We have weddings in Florence, even for foreigners. Of course, the paperwork for non-Italians is a nightmare."

Rafe stole a piece of her pizza with a belated "May I?" after he took a bite. "I've got to order a *Margherita* next time."

She nodded. "It's my go-to pizza. Every time you try a new pizzeria you have to have the simple *Margherita* – no *mozzarella di bufala*, no extra sauce or added garlic – just as it was meant to be. Then you'll know if the place is worth a second visit." She watched him savor the slice. "Now quit stalling. Tell me all."

He wiped his hands on his napkin. "One of the Special Ops guys who pulled me out of the basement in Homs last June was engaged to be married in September. His intended dreamed of a Florentine wedding with all the friends and family. While I was back in Washington last month I was invited to witness the vows in the chamber of a federal judge. Now they're going to party with their nearest and dearest in Florence."

"Fabulous! When's the reception? Where's it being held? A villa in Tuscany? Is the bride also in the military? I'd love to meet the guy who saved your life. Can I…?"

Rafe held up a hand. "Just a minute." He laughed and started to answer her questions. "First, you'll get to meet the whole team. They'll all be here. Second, it's this coming Monday at…"

"Monday!" Caterina interrupted. "Today is Thursday and you are telling me this big party is next Monday? That's not much warning."

Rafe ran a hand over his wavy black hair, cut short at the temples and longer on top. "I just heard it myself this morning. They didn't know I was here, so I wasn't on the guest list. Now that they do know, I've been lassoed in to assist with the last minute details." He gave her a grin. "I was hoping you would help, but maybe with this new case, you're going to be too busy."

"Sure I'll help. Other people are dealing with the details of that poor woman's death. I'm only in the info loop. Also, I'm a resource if they need assistance from one of the consulates. You know, family notification and stuff like that. We still don't know if the victim is Italian or foreign, though I bet she's from Maine. When I get the photos from the coroner, I'll know for sure."

"That's a tragedy."

"No matter who she was, it's a tragedy," she said and then regretted sounding like a scold. She shook her head and gave him a rueful smile.

"Don't I know it." He took a sip of his beer. "Anyway, I won't need you before Saturday. It will be really great having someone who can speak the lingo. I'm sure I could *parlare italiano…*" He saw her raised eyebrow. "Anyway, thanks. Of course, Max and his family are coming up from Rome, but too late for…"

"Max?" Caterina interrupted, again. "You say Max Turner is attending this party?" She and the Legal Attaché with the U.S. Embassy in Rome, had foiled a bomber's plot the week after Easter. Caterina still had a bit of an unrequited crush on Max and he had been instrumental in sending Rafe to Florence to recover from weeks of captivity in an ISIS stronghold in Homs. She never learned why an FBI agent was in Syria and Rafe had not been at all forthcoming. "Does Max know the groom?"

"He met Jake – that's his name, Jacob Miller – when the team dropped me off in Rome. But it's Max's wife, Julia, who knows the couple better. She's from Tennessee and Ross Osborne, Jacob's husband, is the legislative aide for a congresswoman from Tennessee. Julia used to babysit him when she was in high school and he was a toddler."

"Wait, wait, wait, let me get this straight." Caterina could hardly get the words out. "You're saying that the happy couple is two guys and that a bunch of people from Tennessee are descending on Florence this weekend, including a member of the U.S. Congress. And that Max's wife knows the whole crowd."

Rafe seemed to be trying to keep a straight face. "Actually, I don't know about the congresswoman. I figure Jake would have mentioned it if the arrangements included that complexity."

"That's the first thing you should definitely find out. The U.S. Consul General in Florence should be notified. And maybe even the Ambassador in Rome."

"Max will be on top of that. He works at the friggin' embassy. Julia would know if Ross's boss was going to be gracing the festivities with her presence."

Caterina went into planning mode while nibbling on a leftover piece of pizza crust. "Where is the party going to be held?"

"Some museum called the ... what was it?" Rafe pulled out his cell phone and swiped the screen a number of times. "The Stibbert. Museo Stibbert. Strange name. Not very Italian. Do you know of it?"

"Very well. When I was a kid, it was one of my favorites. Now my nephew and niece insist I take them there at least once or twice a year."

Max looked confused as he closed his phone. "It's a kids' museum?"

"No, Museo Stibbert is for adults, too. But when you see it you'll understand the appeal for children. It's a very eccentric place, perfect for a wedding reception. In fact, I think the British Consulate celebrated Queen Elizabeth's birthday there last year." Caterina finished her glass of wine. "So what are they asking you to do?"

"I'm picking up Zandra Brooks tomorrow at the airport. She was Ross's best woman at the nuptials. She's been handling all of the details so far."

"I assume they reserved hotel rooms for everybody. It's not high season, but Florence is still pretty booked in late October."

"Zandra got a block of rooms at the Regency Hotel. It's on the other side of town in some piazza I can't pronounce."

"Piazza Massimo D'Azeglio. I know the hotel. Good choice."

Rafe continued, "Most everybody is already in Italy somewhere or arriving on Saturday. But this is where I need your help."

"Anything – so long as it's not during working hours tomorrow."

"No, we need you the next day, Saturday. Zandra set up a meeting with the Florentine party planner at the museum to go over all of the details. Zandra insists I go along, although what she thinks I know about catering and decorations, I don't know…"

"Rafe, I'd be happy to come," Caterina interjected. "I've got the whole day free."

"And could you help me pick out a gift for the guys? Not anything big. Just something to take home that's made here."

"I know just the place."

CHAPTER EIGHT

Crossing the street along the Arno in front of the gelateria owned by Caterina's friend Sandra, Rafe almost lost his cone with scoops of pistachio and *crema buontalenti* when a Vespa cut the corner at full speed.

"Watch it!" Caterina wasn't sure if she was yelling at the scooter driver or Rafe, who barely missed her foot when he stepped backwards out of the way.

They made it to the other side of the street and were leaning against the wall, watching the dark water rushing by far below, when she said, "You're right, you know." She scooped a small bite of gelato out of the cup cradled in her left hand.

Rafe raised an enquiring brow as he caught a creamy drip on the side of his sugar cone.

"Your friends would never be able to get married in Italy. Even if a majority of the population – and I think some study put the number at fifty-four percent in favor – urged the parliament to make the change for marriage equality, the politicians would never take such a position against the wishes of the Vatican."

Rafe nodded, but said, "Some Catholic countries have legalized same-sex marriage, haven't they?"

She turned her back on the river. "Spain, France and Ireland have all voted for an equal right to marry and they all have a larger proportion of Catholics than any other religion."

"So how does the Vatican hold so much power in Italy and not those countries?"

She scraped the last melted chocolaty gelato up with her tiny plastic spoon. "It's certainly not because Italians are more observant. The churches are mostly empty on Sunday morning. Even Portugal, where Catholics are in the pews, has marriage equality laws. But here we have history and culture and money all working against Italians moving into the 21st century."

"I'm right in thinking that the Vatican doesn't have representatives in the Italian government, aren't I?"

"Vatican City is its own little city-state with its own government. But it is surrounded by Rome and has wielded great political influence throughout history."

"But it can't directly tell the Italian government what to do, or even take an official position, I would guess."

Caterina shook her head as she tossed the gelato cup into a trash barrel at the corner of the bridge and zipped up her jacket against the brisk night wind. "The Pope and the Cardinals can definitely take a public position and they do so both in person or in the press. One of the cardinals said that the marriage equality vote in Ireland was a defeat for humanity and that the Irish were worse than pagans."

"Harsh." Rafe's laugh held no humor. "Good thing excommunication has gone out of style."

"Watch it there." Caterina pointed at the gelato dripping down the back of his cone. "I think the issue is that the wealthy in Italy at least pay lip service to the Vatican and they influence the Prime Minister and the government. Also, though I have no real basis for this, it's just a feeling, but organized crime has something to do with it."

"What do you mean?" He popped the last of his cone in his mouth and wiped his fingers on the small napkin.

"The criminal clans, mostly in the south and Sicily tend to be in areas that are more religiously observant and homophobic. Historically there's a lot of corruption and control of politicians by these criminal groups. I remember my father talking about the years the Christian Democracy Party was in power with Prime Ministers like Giulio Andreotti. He had strong ties to both the crime bosses and the Pope. He was both pious and corrupt."

"But that's not the situation now."

Even though her building was only a hundred feet away, she suggested that they walk the long way around

from bridge to bridge before he would leave her at the
front door. "Now our ever-changing politicians are just
trying to keep the economy afloat and deal with the tidal
wave of North African immigration. They are definitely
not going to address marriage equality any time soon."

"For Jake and Ross that's not a problem. They just
want a great party."

She took his arm. "They are sure to get it. Even if
their party planner is hopeless, the Stibbert Museum is a
party in itself. I can't wait until you see it. I'm going to
have fun just watching your face when you see the
eccentric place. It's definitely not the Uffizi."

They walked in silence for a couple of minutes, until
she thought of something to add to her earlier civics
lesson. "We do have the legal construct of civil unions
and domestic partnerships. Of course, that came about
because Italian men and women are not marrying each
other any more."

"What?" Rafe stopped walking. "Why is that?"

"My guess is that it is still too hard to get divorced.
The Vatican may not agree, but ever since the seventies,
Italians have been very comfortable with couples just
living together. The civil union status helped with
property ownership, taxes and legalizing the kids."

As they strolled onto the Santa Trinita Bridge,
Caterina saw a man, standing on the jutting triangular
pylon, boost a woman over the wall to the sidewalk in
front of them and then levered himself up and over to
join her. As Rafe took her arm to guide her around the
couple, Caterina observed, "That's where we think the
woman on the embankment fell from into the river. It's

not the first time someone ended up in the Arno from this bridge."

"Why not fence it off or set up some sort of barrier? That's what they would do in the U.S.," said Max.

Caterina gave him a mock horrified look. "Fence a historic monument; a bridge designed almost five hundred years ago?" she said, laughing. "That would never be done in Florence."

"Hardly five centuries old," Rafe said. "Even I know that the Germans blew up the original bridge in 1944. This is just a fifty-year-old copy."

Caterina became more serious, slowing to look down into the dark water rushing below as she explained, "It was rebuilt using the original stones pulled from the bottom of the river. Using photographs and the original plans taken from the Florentine archives they reconstructed it as close to the original as possible. The old stones had been quarried where the Boboli Garden is now. For those fragments that could not be recovered, more stones were cut from hillside of the Boboli." She took a breath. "In the U.S., they would have just thrown up a fancy new bridge, maybe employing the skills of some famous architect like Calatrava to memorialize the loss."

"Sorry, sorry, sorry!" Rafe exclaimed, holding his hands up as if to fend off her indignation. "I beg your pardon. You know I love the fact that this place still looks like it did in Michelangelo's time."

Caterina laughed. "Hardly that. Michelangelo would be appalled to see the Renaissance Disneyland his beloved city has become." She started walking again. "Don't worry. I'll quit preaching."

Before they left the bridge, Caterina pointed up to where a bank of clouds was moving across the face of the almost full moon. "I just hope the weather holds for the party. They've been saying that we're in for a rainy week ahead."

CHAPTER NINE

A gust of wind blew rain hard against the magistrate's office window, rattling the open shutters hooked to the outside wall. Caterina looked out, thinking how lucky she had been to arrive at the Questura before the storm swept in from the northwest. Her boss had just explained that his mother's surgery had been delayed until after the weekend.

"I guess it's good news that her cardiac artery is open enough that her procedure could be delayed when another patient in much worse shape was brought in on an emergency basis," he said, but added, "Still I will be more at ease once this is done." He looked down at the paper Caterina put in front of him. "Do you think this woman was so drunk she just rolled off the *pigne del ponte* into the Arno?

"The coroner has not issued his final report, but it looks like that is a definite possibility," said Caterina. "As I was saying, the blood alcohol level in the report you have there is well into the range to have rendered her unconscious. There are no railings on that part of the bridge."

"Let me see the photos." Magistrate Benigni held out his hand.

Caterina slid a photocopy of the dead woman's face and shoulders taken by Oscar the coroner's assistant, and another one of the photo page of Alice Perkin's passport across the expanse of his desk.

He looked back and forth between the two. "You think we have a match?"

"The eye color is the same and even though the dead woman is more of a brunette, they look similar to me. If you take into account some bloating in the coroner's photo, the mouth, nose, and eyebrows are similar. We have a hair brush from the purse from where the passport was also found. The crime lab will take about a week to confirm a DNA match since there is no claim we can make that the work must be expedited."

"What about the Australian in custody? Don't the *polizia* need the DNA confirmation before they can release him?"

"Apparently not. Lt. Capra is planning to let him go today. The coroner provided him with a verbal summary of his findings, saying that there is no evidence of a crime. She wasn't strangled or bludgeoned. The scrape on her forehead wasn't a mortal wound. She wasn't dead before she went into the water. The cause of death was drowning and it was river water in her lungs."

"Hypothetically, Mundt may have pushed her in, but Capra has no proof and there is no obvious motive. An accidental drowning, do you think?"

"Neither Leo nor I could find any connection between Mr. Mundt and Alice Perkins. I think he is going to try to find Ian, the Irishman who Mundt says was with them on the bridge around midnight, but that's a long shot since we have no last name for him. Also, reportedly Ian left the other two much earlier in the night."

"I hope that Capra is going to keep track of Donald Mundt for the rest of his time in Italy, and perhaps longer, in case some other information comes to light."

"I'm sure he will, sir."

The magistrate pushed the photocopies back to her. "This makes it easier for the mayor…," he was saying as a knock sounded on the closed office door. "Come in."

Caterina turned to see Marco Capponi slip into the office. The magistrate nodded toward the empty visitor chair.

"Sit down, Marco. We're almost done here." He turned back to Caterina. "I got a call this morning from the mayor's press secretary. Mayor Moretti is going to make an official statement commending the actions of Adamou Nadja."

"But sir…," Marco started.

His boss ignored the interruption. "Caterina, I would like you to investigate the process by which the mayor can expedite a *permesso di soggiorno* for Mr. Nadja. Does he need a visa first or could we... ?"

"Sir, I must object," said Marco.

"*Object?*" Caterina caught a glimpse Paolo Benigni's glacial expression before he looked down.

"Well, not object, exactly," Marco said as he flushed and dropped his silver pen. After he retrieved it, though, his face was resolute. "It is just that the message of granting residency, even temporarily, out of the normal process, only encourages more illegal immigration."

"How so?" the magistrate asked in a soft tone.

Caterina was not surprised that Marco failed to comprehend the warning as he blustered on. "My work with the antiterrorism task force has brought a heightened understanding of how the African masses coming to our shores are involved in human trafficking, usually leading to prostitution, and an increase in violent crime, like rapes or robbery."

"But you must admit, Marco, that the immigration system as it is administered in this country is largely subjective..."

"But, sir..."

"... and you know nothing about Mr. Nadja's circumstances. Caterina, on the other hand, has a great deal of information, since it is *her* case. I'm sure she would agree with me that if we could convince all refugees arriving in this country to act in the same heroic manner as this young man, we would all be better for it." He turned to Caterina. "As I was saying, please write up a short – about two pages should do it – narrative of Adamou Nadja's background and actions yesterday.

Append a concise step-by-step action memo on how to get legal status for him. Make sure it's on the mayor's desk this afternoon."

He looked back at Marco with a raised eyebrow. "I'm sure once Mayor Moretti is briefed he can explain to the City Council on Monday just how exceptional this visitor to our country is and how deserving he is of being commended and assisted in his stay, be it long or short, in Italy."

Marco was silent.

Caterina gathered her notebook and papers before standing. "Sir, did they inform you whether the mayor wants Mr. Nadja to attend the City Council meeting on Monday?"

"I'm sure the press secretary would like the front page coverage to include a photo of the mayor shaking the hero's hand. Do you think he will be able to stand by then?"

Caterina looked down on the small bald spot on the crown of Marco's head. She knew that he thought of it as his only defect and worked unsuccessfully to cover it with the surrounding strands and a bit of hair gel. She pulled her focus back to the magistrate's question.

"I expect so, sir. I will keep you updated." Caterina was grinning as she left the office, happier than she should have been, knowing that Marco had been taken down a peg. Over her shoulder she added, "I will also try to find the family, if any, of Alice Perkins from Maine. If the woman from the Arno is her, the U.S. Consul General may want us to assist with the notification of her next of kin."

Before leaving the Questura for the U.S. Consulate, Caterina tried to call her mother to tell her that Marcella Fontana-Benigni was going to have a medical procedure and was stuck in the hospital over the weekend. The two women were not the closest of friends, but they did serve on a number of committees together. She knew her mother would express severe displeasure if she heard the news from another source.

Margaret Mary did not answer her cell phone. Oh well, Caterina thought, I'll drop into the Osteria for lunch after I find out what I can about Alice Perkins' family.

CHAPTER TEN

Osteria da Guido was full with a line of waiting customers despite the afternoon's cold rain. Caterina pulled open the door and walked into the warm dining room redolent with the smell of pasta sauce and roast meat. She looked for her father and spied his broad back as he talked to customers at a table near the front window. She stopped on her way to the back of the Osteria to chat briefly with Gino Buonamici, one of the regulars who ate lunch at the same small table on either Thursday or Friday for as long as she could remember. Soon she was taking a chair at the large table, reserved for the family, outside the swinging door to the kitchen. She expected to find her mother there, but the table was unoccupied.

She pulled out her cell phone and was flipping through her text messages when Lorenzo, her older brother, pushed out of the kitchen backwards carrying two steaming flat bowls of *ravioli ai funghi porcini con burro e salvia*. Caterina breathed in the rich aroma of butter, mushrooms and sage.

Before she could comment, Lorenzo said, "*La Mamma* is looking for you. She just left."

"And I wanted to talk to her," said Caterina. "I just can't remember why."

"Think about it while I drop these off." He headed across the room to a table where two men in suits sat sharing a half liter carafe of red wine.

The magistrate's mother, Caterina recalled. That's what she wanted to tell her mother about. Margaret Mary would certainly want to make a hospital visit to her old acquaintance.

She noticed a missed call on her phone from Patricia Benvenuti, the magistrate's administrative assistant. It must have come through while she was at the U.S. Consulate, researching Alice Perkins and briefing the Consul General's assistant. The security guard insisted all cell phones be powered off while inside the building. She touched the call back link on the screen. Patricia answered.

"Pat, it's Caterina. Sorry I missed your call. What's up?"

Patricia, speaking Italian infused with her native Australian accent, told her that she needed to drop by the apartment of a couple of French students that afternoon for the purpose of interviewing them and discussing the likely outcome of the theft of items from their apartment that had occurred the night before.

"Were they home when the break-in happened?" Caterina asked as Lorenzo stopped back at the table miming, *What do you want to eat?* She shrugged.

"It seems not. The police report says they were at the disco in the Cascine Park until late and didn't notice anything was gone until this morning. The magistrate just got the report an hour ago. The officer who did the initial interview didn't speak French, of course, and the girls only have beginner Italian, so thus the need for a visit. I gave them a quick call and told them you would be by this afternoon."

"Okay. Text me the address and a cell phone number for at least one of them. I'm going to have some lunch at my father's place and then I'll go."

"The apartment is on Via Taddea behind the *Mercato Centrale* so it will be on your way back to the Questura," Patricia said and then added, "Give my regards to your father."

"I will and please tell the magistrate that I found information for Alice Perkins' father. He lives in Vermont. She also has a brother, but I couldn't find an address or phone number for him."

After they said their goodbyes and as Caterina was disconnecting the call, her brother reappeared from the kitchen with a bowl of *tagliatelle* coated with melted butter and topped with a small mound of shaved white truffles. He placed the bowl in front of her.

"There is nothing better on the menu today," he said.

Caterina leaned over the pasta to savor the full aroma of the truffles. She could never find the words to describe the scent, but she thought it was one of the sexiest food smells ever.

"Mmmm, *gnam, gnam*," she said. "Ambrosia, Renzo. Thanks. Perfect for a rainy day."

"Perfect for *any* day," said their father, who pulled out a chair and sat across from her. "I think I was able to bargain Gianluca down to the lowest price he would accept, but I still had to promise him my next two children." Cosimo Falcone's laugh boomed across the dining room.

Caterina chuckled with him as she picked up a fork and nodded her thanks to her brother for the glass of red wine and small carafe he placed on the table. "Good thing you're through with the whole procreation thing, Babbo."

"Good thing he didn't ask for my future grandchildren," Cosimo retorted. "I'm sure he wouldn't go after Lorenzo's brood, but some day I'm sure you, *principessa mia*, will…"

"Don't go there, Babbo. I don't want anything to mar the experience of my first bite of this season's white truffles." She took a bite, chewed in silence, swallowed and took a small sip of wine. They both watched her, waiting. "Perfect. I only wish you could figure out how to make truffles last for more than a month or two."

Lorenzo snorted. "They only last for five or six days. The moment they are dug up, they start losing flavor. *Mangia! Mangia!*" He returned to the kitchen, dodging one of the waiters as she came through the door with a platter topped with a two-inch thick, perfectly grilled, *bistecca alla fiorentina* raised high on her right hand and a carafe of red wine clutched by the neck in her left one. "*Scusa mi*, Marti!" he said, as he disappeared through the swinging door.

Cosimo picked up the carafe and poured himself an inch of wine in the second glass his son had provided. "I told your mother that *faraona* would be good for Sunday. I picked up some Brussels sprouts and new potatoes to roast with the birds."

"Perfect. It sounds like you don't need me until we sit down to eat. I can sleep in."

Cosimo frowned. "I suppose, but you know I always appreciate your company in the kitchen. Your mother … well…"

Caterina grinned. "I know, Babbo, but think of all of the other talents she has." She twirled another fork full of pasta against the side of the bowl.

Her father, belying his bulk, stood and wove quickly through the tables to escort a set of what Caterina thought of as "the ladies who lunch" regulars out the door, opening each of their umbrellas to save their perfectly coifed hair from ruin.

Although the Osteria was kept afloat by the patronage of tourists who read about it on travel blogs and in international travel magazines, Caterina loved the fact that there were always tables filled with residents, craftsmen, and shopkeepers of the neighborhood. But the regulars were aging and the new generations were not so interested in a sit-down lunch and would rather have pizza at night. Caterina wondered if her father would change his mind and reopen on Sunday when Florentine families traditionally went out for lunch together.

When he came back to the Falcone family table, it was as if no time had passed. "Speaking of talent, *tesoro* … I hear that the mayor is talking about you again."

"What?" She smiled, not paying much attention, as Lorenzo came back with a small salad of radicchio greens, dressed with olive oil and lemon, and a basket of bread.

"It's about you and that African fellow."

Lorenzo stopped, his hand on the kitchen door, waiting for his father to continue.

"Oh, that," said Caterina, wiping the last bit of pasta sauce with a *scarpetta* of bread.

"What African?" asked her brother.

Cosimo explained. "Taddeo Toddi, the mayor's press secretary, was in for lunch and said that his boss is doing some sort of keys-to-the-city thing for that guy Caterina pulled out of the river yesterday." He put on a mock frown. "And why am I hearing about my daughter's exploits from a political hack, was all I could think, so I didn't hear the details."

Caterina laughed as she pushed her pasta bowl toward Lorenzo and picked up a clean fork to start her salad. "One, no 'exploits' were involved. Two, Taddeo Toddi is not a hack. And three, it's not the keys to the city … or at least I don't think so … it's a *permesso di soggiorno*, so hopefully the poor man will be legal after risking…"

Lorenzo interrupted. "I heard about this from one of the cooks. He talked to the *vigile* who was keeping people off the *lungarno* yesterday. They said the guy was no hero, but probably was trying to cover up a murder. That's more believable."

Caterina pushed away her salad plate with more force than she expected. It spun across the table where her father caught it. She glared at her brother. "What do you mean, Renzo?"

"Those illegal scum are ruining this country. Just last week, two Moroccans and a guy from Sudan robbed a couple of tourists on a beach near Pesaro and then raped the woman in front of her husband."

"Don't edit the story to fit your needs, Lorenzo," said Caterina in a tight low voice. "Those 'Moroccans' were the teenage sons of an Italian woman and a Moroccan man, born and raised in Italy. Citizens. Italians. I think it was even *their father* who turned them in."

"But the Sudanese ringleader?"

"He is an asylum-seeker with a *permesso*. He's been living in Italy for three years." She took a deep breath and finished her glass of wine. "I'm not saying that they are not guilty, but you can't blame those crimes on race."

Lorenzo turned to leave, his parting words thrown over his shoulder. "Even you have to admit they bring filth and chaos to Florence."

"Tourists bring filth and chaos to Florence," Caterina snapped back at him a bit too loudly.

Her father stepped between her and the dining room. "Some of those tourists speak Italian, too," he said in a low tone. "And they enjoy a quiet lunch in my osteria."

Caterina wasn't going to concede. "How did you raise such a racist son, Babbo? Next he's going to support the Northern League with all the other neo-fascists."

"Nationalists, not fascists," Cosimo said automatically, but then appeared to realize that didn't help. He put his large hand on her shoulder. *"Tesoro, con calma."*

"I can't calm down," she said, shrugging him away. "This kind of knee-jerk anti-immigration drivel makes me sick." She stood, grabbed her purse and phone, and looked up at her father's troubled face. "Adamou Nadja is a real hero. He risked his life. He deserves a break and the mayor is doing the right thing."

The rain did nothing to improve Caterina's mood as she crossed the river on the Santa Trinita Bridge, trying not to knock umbrellas with a Chinese tour group that numbered about forty by her estimate. She was taller than most of them, so her left shoulder was thoroughly soaked from the water rolling off their umbrellas as they passed.

The two French girls were waiting in their apartment, as Patricia had told her they would be. Both were nineteen and studying economics at the European Research Institute in Fiesole, a small town located on a ridge overlooking Florence.

They explained that since they lived on the third floor of the building, they didn't think it was necessary to lock their windows when they were out of the apartment.

"We always make sure all three locks on the door were secure, even when we are here," said Celine Plantier.

Her flat mate, Viviane Genet, asked, "What if we had been home, asleep when they came in?"

Caterina explained that it was not uncommon for thieves to target students by watching them come and go and then to walk across the terracotta roofline to access a top floor apartment from the wide stone sill through an open window. "They don't plan a break-in while you are home and they are fast. It probably took less than five minutes."

"But wouldn't someone see them?" Viviane asked.

"It was probably one or two men who came in, after dark, wearing black clothes. What was taken?"

"Our laptops and Celine's Samsung tablet."

Celine added, "They also took a gold necklace with an opal pendant that my grandmother gave me."

Caterina paused in taking notes, "That's probably harder to bear than the loss of the computers."

"Maybe." Celine gave a wry smile. "But my thesis is on the computer and I was stupid enough not to back it up to the cloud or put it on a pen drive."

Caterina winced, adding, "Probably just one guy came in and there was another on the roof, lifting things up and putting them into a backpack." She stopped writing and looked at both of them sitting side-by-side on the slipcovered couch behind an Ikea coffee table. "I'm so so sorry this happened and I hate to tell you that you probably won't get anything back. I'm sure you tried any 'find my phone' type apps you have." They nodded. "The police will be checking all of the usual places, but these type of thieves usually have perfected the process of fencing the electronics within hours."

Caterina gave the students her standard list of suggestions for securing their valuables, apartment, and personal security in Florence with additional detailed information on how to avoid pickpockets. She urged them to always be with friends when they were outside after dark.

As she walked on to the Questura, Caterina remembered when Florence had been safe, if not crime-free, when she was the same age as the French students. She wouldn't allow herself to think that the influx of undocumented refugees had made the streets less safe and brought in a new criminal class, but she had to admit that it probably hadn't improved the situation.

CHAPTER ELEVEN

Caterina didn't button her raincoat as she stepped out the massive front door of her apartment building on Saturday morning. The sun shone brightly on the *Ponte Santa Trinita* as she walked to the city center. It was unseasonably warm and humid. The reason for the coat was the steep bank of blue-gray cumulous clouds that towered over the northern hills. The forecast was dire. She tucked a small umbrella and scarf into her coat pocket and hoped she hadn't made a mistake by wearing white tennis shoes.

As she entered *Piazza della Repubblica*, she saw Rafe standing by the merry-go-round, talking to a woman of medium height wearing a tank top that displayed her muscular arms and neck. She had café latte skin and black hair cut short around her ears, but gelled straight up on top. Rafe was in his usual black t-shirt and black jeans.

"Caterina," called Rafe, waving her over. "This is Zandra Brooks."

Caterina shook Zandra's proffered hand, thinking that even though she topped the woman by six inches and outweighed her by fifteen pounds, in a fight the American would best her anytime. She stopped mid-thought, wondering why that would even come to mind. Maybe because Zandra's bare arms were so chiseled and her shoulders were so broad.

"Thanks for helping us out with the reception," Zandra said. "I'm sure the party planner has it under control, but I'm a bit obsessive when it comes to the details."

Caterina laughed. "I'm a bit that way myself and considering that you have all of these out-of-towners to organize, it would be nice not to worry about the canapés and Prosecco."

"Right you are."

Caterina pointed to the empty taxi stand on the other side of the piazza. "The Stibbert is not in the historic center and I figure that you don't want to hassle with the bus, so let's grab a cab. There should be one coming along soon."

As they stood outside the Café Concerto Paskowski, one of the four historic cafés inside the square, Caterina heard her name being called. She turned to scan the nearby tables.

"*Mio Dio*, how did they meet?" she said under her breath, but not low enough to escape Rafe's ears.

"Who?" he asked, looking around.

"Give me a moment," she muttered.

"No rush," he said, but then he followed her to one of the café's outside tables where a plump blonde woman in a lacy peach blouse sat across from a brunette with incredible long legs, displayed to their full advantage by a very short black leather skirt and very high red stilettos. The blonde was waving at Caterina, but her tablemate had yet to turn around.

"Melissa, how *nice* to see you," said Caterina as she glanced back over her shoulder to see Rafe two steps behind her. "I had no idea you knew Veronique."

A slender hand with long nails polished in the exact red of the shoes was extended to Caterina, but Veronique's eyes went immediately to Rafe. "And who is this — what do they say — long drink of water? Is that what they say, Melissa?" Her accented English was vaguely British, with overtones of Eastern Europe.

"Very good, Veronique. But in Texas '*tall* drink of water' is what we usually say," Melissa answered, emphasizing her Texas twang. "He certainly fits the description." Her blue eyes swept Rafe from top to toe.

Caterina was amused to watch his face pink up. Serves him right for following me, she thought.

Zandra Brooks joined the group, stepping around Rafe to see better.

"*Ispettore* Falcone," Veronique switched to Italian. "Please introduce me to your friends and tell me how you know the lovely Melissa."

"Zandra Brooks, Rafe Mathews, may I introduce Veronique from Moscow," Caterina complied in English. "And Melissa Kincaid from Dallas."

"Zandra," mused Veronique, tapping one crimson finger nail against her lower lip. "An English name meaning 'defender of men.' It suits you, even though you don't look very British."

"All American," Zandra said, holding out her hand. "Though with a Latino Afro-American father and an Irish mother."

"So that's where the light green eyes come from," said Veronique. "And what about you, big guy?"

"All American, as well," said Rafe. "I…"

"I remember *you*," exclaimed Melissa. "Boy, have you bulked up." She jumped up and kissed his cheek. "You were skeletal when we met a few months ago. I thought you had some terminal…"

Caterina interrupted, aware that the exuberant Texan recalled that Rafe, just out of his ordeal in Homs, had assisted in the search when Melissa was kidnapped in July. "But you didn't answer *my* question, Melissa. How did you meet Veronique?"

Melissa giggled. "I was standing near her table, waiting for Davide. And she leaned over and commented on my blouse. She liked the design, but said it was wrong for the season. Peach, I guess gets put away by mid-September. Who knew? She suggested aubergine for October, especially with my hair and skin tones."

"Veronique was always good at fashion advice," said Caterina, sarcasm barely veiled.

Veronique nodded. "Yes, and those white sport shoes are all wrong, not only are they for summer, but in a couple of hours they will get filthy when it starts raining."

"Thanks, Veronique." Caterina turned to go.

"And I see that your mother hasn't convinced you to cut your hair."

Caterina couldn't control her hand in its compulsive need to check the auburn curls escaping the loose braid. She spoke over the Russian's advice to "always listen to your mother" with the timely observation, "There's a taxi. We've got to go." She added, "Melissa, give my regards to Davide. Veronique, don't get her involved in any of your schemes."

Laughter followed the threesome to the waiting car. Caterina and Rafe took the window seats with Zandra in the middle. After Caterina gave the driver directions, she sat back with a long sigh.

"There's more than one story there, I'll bet," said Rafe. "Of course, I remember Melissa. Weren't she and that cook engaged or something?"

"Davide Johnson," Caterina agreed with a nod. "They got married last month. It was just before you got back from Washington."

Zandra wasn't interested in Melissa's marital state. "She's a he, right?"

Rafe turned from looking out the window at a Vespa that almost clipped the side mirror. "What?"

"It's the shoes. If he wants to hide the fact, he can't wear cherry red heels. Black would be better."

"Veronique, aka Vladimir Markov, isn't hiding," said Caterina. "She's part of a long tradition of exotic Florentine transvestites." She shook her head. "I would never have guessed that those two would cross paths. I suppose it is inevitable that now that they realize that they both know me, they will compare stories."

"Stories about what?" asked Rafe.

"Veronique was a person of interest in that bombing last Easter. You know – the one Max and I worked on."

"You know Max?" Zandra interjected.

"In a professional capacity," said Caterina, blushing. "You, too?"

"He taught a class at Quantico when I was there." the American woman said and then asked, "But where does Melissa come in? Same case?"

"No," said Caterina. "She became a thorn in my side during a murder investigation this past summer. The killing of a British student."

"How did a middle-aged woman from Dallas get mixed up in the murder of a Brit?"

"She found the body."

"Oh no," said Zandra at the same time Rafe said, "I remember why she was a pain." He let Caterina tell the story.

"She started channeling her inner Nancy Drew," Caterina said wrapping up the tale. She looked out her window and saw that their cab had already passed the train station and was circling the walls of a large edifice. She changed the subject, leaving Melissa and Veronique behind.

"That's the *Fortezza da Basso*, one of the two 16th century forts built on orders of the Medici clan to protect the wealthy of Florence in times of war and siege." She pointed to a wide street with four official traffic lanes that seemed to be accommodating six lanes of actual traffic. "We're coming up to the ring road around the city, which used to be where the last major wall stood. The wall was destroyed in the 1800s to make the road. So you see the Stibbert villa would have been outside the walled city in one of the ancient suburbs. In Stibbert's time, his home was know as the Villa of Montughi."

"Frederick Stibbert was British wasn't he?" asked Zandra. "I've been reading up on the museum."

"His father was English, kind of the black sheep of his family. He was about sixty when he settled in Florence. Frederick's mother was from a small hill town north of the city and was in her thirties when Thomas Stibbert married her. Rumor has it that she was his housekeeper."

"Got her in a family way," mused Zandra.

"Maybe." Caterina nodded. "This was sometime around 1830. Old Thomas died when Frederick was nine and had already been sent to boarding school in London."

"A great British tradition," said Rafe.

"I can't imagine how his Italian mother handled that," said Caterina. "But she didn't bring him home immediately. He stayed at school in England until he turned twenty-one and came into a huge inheritance from his grandfather, who made his fortune in colonial India."

The taxi took them through a quiet neighborhood and at the base of a steep tree-covered ridge, turned up a narrow street past a walled park, to arrive at a highly-decorated villa painted a golden yellow with the traditional terra cotta roof. "Stibbert's villa," Caterina said, "His mother's, actually. She bought it after her husband died. Frederick came here when he left university at Cambridge."

As they got out of the cab, Rafe passed Caterina a twenty euro bill to pay the driver. She returned with a couple of euro coins in change.

Zandra walked to the low terrace wall overlooking the expansive gardens. "Jake and Ross are going to love this. What a place to have a party." Just then large drops of rain spilled out of billowing gray clouds. They rushed to the entrance of the Stibbert Museum.

CHAPTER TWELVE

Three tourists from Edinburgh and a Florentine couple with their nine-year-old son milled around in front of the ticket counter as Rafe and Zandra, followed by Caterina, approached down the narrow dark entry hall.

The ticket-taker smiled and said in English, "The next tour starts in five minutes. Would you like to join this group?"

Caterina answered in Italian, "We have a meeting scheduled with Beatrice Forzoni at eleven. We were told to meet her here."

The young woman's smile widened and she switched languages. "Bea is up in the café. If you just wait until this group leaves on their tour, I'll take you up there by the backstairs. Or if you know the way around via the outside terrace, you can go now."

"I know where the café is, but it's starting to rain so we will wait for you to take us by the inside route," said Caterina.

Ten minutes later, they were traversing underground corridors, passing through two large rooms. "These were the *cantina* and wine cellar of the villa." Caterina translated what their escort said for the other two, adding, "This isn't open to visitors to the museum." They climbed a narrow stone stairway and went through a door into a small coffee bar.

A striking blond woman with straight defined black brows over a retro-designed pair of red eye glasses sat at one of the small tables. Her hair swung straight, cut in a sharp angle from the nape of her neck to brush her collar bone in front. She wore a red silk blouse open to the third button, a narrow black wool skirt, and polished high-heeled black knee-high boots with a subtle designer logo incorporated into gold chains at each ankle.

She looked up as they entered, seeming to assess each of them. She stood and held her hand out to Zandra and said with a slightly Florentine-inflected British accent, "You must be Ms. Brooks. I am Beatrice. Pleased to meet you."

Zandra took her hand, saying, "Likewise. I've got to say I love those boots."

"Thank you," said Bea, glancing at one foot briefly. She turned to Rafe, "And you are one of the grooms?"

"Nope, just a helpful friend," he answered, adding, "This is…"

"I know Ms. Falcone," Bea Forzoni interjected. "*Piacere*," she greeted Caterina.

"*Piacere*," Caterina responded in kind. "Have we met?" she added in English as she took the soft cool hand Bea offered.

"You attended the opera gala with your mother last May. The Maggio Musicale Fiorentino's opening night. *Il Barbiere di Siviglia*. I organized the after-party."

Caterina remembered the night mostly for her mother's insistence that she wear a pair of strappy sandals that gave her blisters, although she also recalled that the opera had been first-rate. "It was a beautiful evening and the opera was sublime."

Bea gestured to her table. "Let's sit and go over the arrangements. I think everything is set although we may need some weather-related contingencies." They all looked out the glass door of the café where the rain was creating large puddles in the gravel courtyard.

After they were seated, she passed a typewritten sheet of paper to Zandra. "Here is a copy of the contract for you. The wire transfer of payment-in-full was deposited in my account last Wednesday." She opened a folder and took out a smaller piece of paper. "Here is the receipt for the funds."

"Will we be able to walk through the villa today?" asked Zandra as she tucked the paperwork into her leather satchel.

"Of course," said Beatrice. "As we discussed, the villa will be completely open for ninety minutes before the dinner is served. During that time, guests will be allowed full access to the museum. I estimate one hour for the scavenger hunt itself and thirty minutes to herd the stragglers from the museum into the ballroom. Only the ballroom, the adjoining corridor and the Peacock Room will be accessible while dinner is served. The rest of the museum will be closed."

"Ballroom, Peacock Room – it sounds so romantic," said Zandra.

"The Peacock Room used to be the men's smoking room in Frederick Stibbert's day. Of course, now that won't be allowed, but the outside terrace will be open, weather permitting. We will also serve an *aperitivo* – Prosecco, canapés, and Negroni punch – on the terrace as guests arrive. If it is raining, we will transfer the pre-dinner gathering to a new portion of the museum where all of the exhibits are behind glass, so there is no danger from spillage."

Bea and Zandra discussed the menu and the cake, as Rafe and Caterina sat back, just listening. Finally, Bea closed her folder and stood. "I believe you liked my idea of a scavenger hunt through the museum during the hour before dinner."

Caterina laughed. "Not the type of hunt where people actually collects things, I hope."

"No, the 'collecting' is done by taking photos with cell phones," Beatrice responded with a tight smile. "I did this for a group of Americans from San Francisco last month and it worked out quite well. It makes people look at the museum more closely. And, of course, we have assistants in each room to offer help, although some of them do not speak a lot of English. I try to hire all of the museum's guides for the evening, but a few extra people will be needed to provide sufficient coverage."

Bea took them on an abbreviated tour of the museum, saying, "I don't want to ruin the fun for you the evening of the party. Don't you agree, Caterina?"

"Absolutely," she responded, waving an arm to encompass the Louis XVI parlor from its Aubusson carpet, past the crowd of gilded French chairs, couches and side tables, up along the walls crammed with portraits, some of Stibbert's family and others notable only in the 1700s, to the ceiling sporting pink angels and an elaborate chandelier. "This is just a taste of what you will see the evening of the party. You should experience it for the first time with your friends."

Bea nodded. "For example, Frederick and his mother created this room in 1871 during one of the frequent renovations of the villa." They moved onto a landing above a curved staircase. The wall on one side was covered with a large tapestry and on the other side glass cases were filled with religious reliquaries and vestments. Bea continued, "Wealthy and brilliant, Frederick was an international financier, habitual traveler and passionate collector. This all contributed to the realization of the greatest project of his life: transforming the Villa of Montughi into a museum. This goal drove his every action for fifty years. In his last Will and Testament, he left the museum to the British Government, with the obligation to keep the collection in Florence and to establish the museum in his name. In case of withdrawal by the British, the bequest passed to the municipality of Florence, as actually happened in 1908."

"Did he marry an Italian like his father?" asked
Zandra.

"He had an active social and cultural life, both in
Florence and in London, but he never married," Bea said
as she led them through room after room of armor and
weapons, dating from the Middle Ages to the 1800s. "He
was popular with both men and women. He was known
to be a bit of a dandy, appearing frequently in London's
social magazine *Vanity Fair*. But he was devoted to his
mother."

"Passionate about swords and guns, but he also had
agents out buying up portraits of the rich and famous of
the 16th and 17th centuries," laughed Caterina. "You can
see why I loved this place when I was a kid. I still visit
almost every year."

Rafe whistled at a wall of sabers, "He was definitely
focused on the military – perfect for a party of Navy
Seals."

Bea nodded, "That is what is unique about the
collection. He consulted with the armories of the British
monarchs and those in the Middle East and Asia,
especially Japan." She pointed out a daguerreotype
photograph from the turn of the century of Stibbert
wearing armor standing beside a horse. "He was also
passionate about horses and owned a stable of
thoroughbreds. In 1866, he took part in the Third Italian
War for Independence with Garibaldi's troops and was
awarded a silver medal for his valor during the battle of
the Trentino.

"An adventurer, but attached to his mother," observed Zandra. "More Italian, than English, I think. Did he have siblings?"

Bea nodded. "His sister Sophronia married into the noble Pandolfini family and was famous for her gardens and orchid house. Erminia, his only other sibling, apparently died young and disappeared in history."

When they emerged onto the terrace, the rain had stopped. Bea called a taxi for them and disappeared back into the museum.

They were almost back to the center of Florence when Caterina remembered and said, "You two wanted to do a bit of shopping for the grooms, right?"

"That would be great, but it's starting to pour again," said Rafe. "Not exactly great for wandering around from place to place."

"I'm thinking of just one workshop. Hopefully, it'll stop raining by the time we're done."

"I'm giving Jake and Ross spa certificates for massages Monday afternoon so they're relaxed for the party," Zandra said. "But I'd love to tag along. My mother is watching my three-year-old son back in Chattanooga. I've got to bring her back something nice."

Caterina directed the driver to Via Corso where they got out and hurried down an alley to a door set in the wall across from the ancient church of Santa Margherita dei Cerchi, otherwise known as Dante's Church.

"There's actually no evidence Dante ever went to that church, but it did exist in the 13th century and the present priest is a great marketer of Dante's unrequited love for Beatrice. The donations he gets from romantics are huge," Caterina said, dryly. She opened the door next to a display window filled with jewelry boxes and picture frames. "This is my friend Simone's place. He's the third generation of leather workers."

She greeted the tall slender man with wavy black hair shot with silver, wearing a blue smock. He had been polishing a large red leather picture frame, but put it down, rubbing his hands on a polish-stained rag. "Caterina! *Accidenti*, it's been so long," he said in Florentine dialect. They talked for a minute while Rafe and Zandra looked in the display cases in the small shop.

"These are my friends, Rafe and Zandra. They are actually shopping, not just curious," Caterina said in English. The master craftsman greeted the Americans, also in English.

"Simone's boxes are completely made of leather, except for the large jewelry boxes that require lock and key set in wood, but then covered with fine calfskin. His picture frames also have a wood core, " Caterina explained. "On average there are thirty-two steps and twenty days of work in each small or medium-sized box."

Simone interrupted, "The large and baroque-style boxes require forty steps and fifty days because of the extra layers of leather and the complexity of the design." He picked up a large box with an elegant wave in the lid and opened it to show the leather core and interior.

"Each box starts with a wooden form on which dampened rawhide is bound and allowed to dry," Caterina continued pointing at a pile of thick beige rawhide. "Where the edges meet, Simone must shave the leather thin so that no joint is visible. The top and bottom of the form is covered with separate pieces of rawhide, completing the inner core of the box. Once the thick leather is completely dry, a thin supple layer of beige calfskin is attached with a natural paste and the edges are again shaved with a knife so that no seam shows."

Rafe had a small box in his hands, examining the edges. He looked up with a laugh, "Your friend should hire you to market his wares."

Caterina punched him lightly in the shoulder, "I just know the difference between real art and the stuff made in Morocco or China."

Simone finished the explanation, "The box, once dry, is dyed with a lanolin dye and burnished with a hot smooth steel hand tool applied with great pressure not once, but twice, over the entire box to bring a shine to the leather and enrich the color. Then the sides are cut to create a natural leather hinge." He showed the three-sided opening on a green leather box. "This allows the top to come free and I can remove the wooden form. The edges are finished and all it needs is a final polish."

"My mother would love one of these," said Zandra as she took a photograph with her phone of Simone holding one of his boxes. "Especially since I've met the designer and craftsman. That's so rare these days."

CHAPTER THIRTEEN

Caterina pulled the cork out of a bottle of Barolo and set it aside to breathe, as she finished telling her parents about the previous day's activities. "Jake, one of the grooms, loves playing poker so Rafe got them a leather box for two packs of cards and then, another box about the same size for Ross's political pins and Jake's military award bars, or cuff links and the like." She carried wine glasses to the table. "Zandra got her mother a small box, a ruby-colored leather case for her glasses and one of those little Florentine coin purses that Simone makes, which she thinks her mother will use to store earrings when she travels."

Sitting on a kitchen stool, watching her husband cook, Margaret Mary nodded. "Simone is one of the last true leather craftsmen in Florence. After the flood in '66, so many took the government help and never reopened their destroyed workshops. Simone must have been just a kid, but his father and grandfather stuck it out and he is carrying on the tradition."

Cosimo cut up autumn vegetables – potatoes, turnips, Brussels sprouts, cloves of garlic, and carrots – tossed them in olive oil, salt and coarse ground pepper. "His grandfather's workshop was in the Oltrarno. He used to eat lunch each day in my father's osteria. A classic Florentine gentleman." He added some hot pepper flakes and put the large pan into the oven, turning the heat a bit higher.

"I forgot to tell you that Lorenzo called earlier. He said he's not going to be here for lunch. He's bringing Cosimino and Annamaria over, but he's not staying."

Margaret Mary seemed to take her son's absence at lunch as a personal affront, thought Caterina. But it was actually her father who would be more upset, she knew. He recently chose to shut the osteria on Sunday to guarantee that he would have the family around his table at least once a week.

"What is going on with your brother, Catherine?"

"Don't ask me, mother. He works with Babbo every day. Ask him."

"I have asked him." Margaret Mary slid off her stool and walked over to the sliding glass door to pull the drapes shut, blocking out the relentless gray rain.

"Leave the boy alone," Cosimo said, slicing a crusty loaf of Tuscan bread. "He's allowed some private time and we still get to have lunch with both of our grandchildren." He changed the subject, making Caterina think that he knew more about Lorenzo's plans than he was sharing. "*Tesoro*, where did Rafe find these friends?"

"What friends?"

Cosimo had a look on his face that made Caterina think that he wished he had stayed with the subject of his son's absence. But he continued, "The two guys who got married. Doesn't seem to be the type of people he would know well."

"Well Babbo, one of the *grooms* is a Navy Seal and Ross, the other *groom*, is the chief of staff to a member of the U.S. Congress. The Navy Seal, whose name is Jake, risked his life to be part of the rescue mission that saved Rafe in Syria a few months ago. Remember how skinny and sick-looking he was in August. He had been held captive and starved, and probably worse, for over a month."

"Hmm," said her father, as the front door to the apartment opened and his grandchildren rushed in.

"Nonno! Nonna! We're here!" Annamaria ran into the kitchen and wrapped her chubby arms around her grandfather's leg. He wiped his hands on the towel tied around his waist and picked her up, as his wife said, "No need to scream, darling. Cosimino remember to leave your shoes at the door. Your *pantofole* are there waiting for you."

Without a word, her grandson turned back to find his slippers. Cosimo set Annamaria down and nudged her to the door and her fuzzy bunny pair. Caterina looked down at her own heeled leather slip-ons with crystal accents – her mother's selection.

"Where is your father?" asked Mary Margaret.

Cosimino came back to the kitchen door. "He dropped us at the door downstairs." His Florentine dialect contrasted with her perfect Boston-accented Italian.

"Where was he going?"

"He says he is on a secret mission. Like *Mission Impossible*."

Caterina laughed, "How do you know about *Mission Impossible*?"

"It's a movie, Zia Caterina," Cosimino said in all seriousness. "I saw it at Luigi's house. It's *incredibile*!"

"Set the table, *piccolino*," Caterina said before her mother could question him further about either his movie choices or his father's Sunday plans. "It's too bad we can't eat on the terrace, but it's been raining all night and it's still coming down."

Cosimino set a stack of plates on the table and turned, his face lit with excitement, "Zia, you should see how high the Arno's getting. My friend Gio says it's going to flood into the streets."

"It is not going to flood," said his grandfather at the same time Annamaria said, "How am I going to get to school tomorrow, if the streets are full of water?"

"It is not going to flood," Caterina and her mother said in unison. Caterina handed her niece the breadbasket to put on the table. She turned to Margaret Mary, asking,

"Mother, do you know Beatrice Forzoni? She worked on the Maggio opera gala."

"Of course, I know her. Or, at least, I know her mother. She is a Pesaro of the Venetian Pesaros. They go back to one of the Doges in the 1600s. She married Pierluigi Forzoni, the head of BDV Properties. He has residential and commercial real estate throughout Tuscany."

"So why is Beatrice in the party planning business?"

"Pierluigi does not think women are capable of understanding the complexities of the real estate business, but don't turn your nose up at event planners." She ignored her daughter's protest. "Beatrice mixes only with the best, working only with a select clientele. Didn't you say a member of Congress is coming to the wedding?"

"It's not a wedding. That took place in Washington weeks ago. This is just the reception and I don't think the Congresswoman is coming, but maybe the referral did come through the U.S. Consulate."

"See what I mean? The opera board is the height of respectability. I hear she's chairing the mayor's task force to attract Middle and Far East tourism. An event at the Museo Stibbert is only open to a few planners. She orchestrated the fundraiser for restoration of *La Fontana di Nettuno* that I went to at the Accademia just last month."

Cosimino dropped a pile of silverware on the table with a crash. "Can I come to the party at the Stibbert?" He was hopping up and down with excitement. "I love the Stibbert!"

"I know you do, *tesoro*," said Caterina, sorting the silverware and setting each place. "But this is a party only for adults."

"But it's a museum for kids," her nephew argued.

"Big people can like kid stuff, too, you know? How about if I take you and your sister to the Stibbert on the next weekend you are with your father? We might even ask him to join us."

"Do we have to take Annamaria? She's so slow."

"Am not," screeched his sister.

"Hush, *bambina*," urged Caterina. "Of course we are going to take you, too."

"I like the horses," Annamaria said.

"Me, too. Now, I see that your nonno has put the *faraona e verdure* on the table. Sit in your chair. Napkins down. Time to eat!"

Later, Margaret Mary took Caterina aside. "The one thing you should probably know about Beatrice Forzoni is that her brother Ippolito died in a horrible accident last year."

"What kind of accident?"

"It was some kind of car accident on the *viale* near the *Fortezza da Basso*."

"How awful. How old was he?"

"Nineteen or twenty. He was younger than Beatrice."

"How come I never heard about this accident? Traffic fatalities are not that common in Florence."

"I think you were in Paris on that Interpol training program. That was last year, wasn't it?" When Caterina nodded, Margaret Mary added, "They say Ippolito's death broke his father. Pierluigi is one of those patriarchal types who feels that his son was the heir apparent to his real estate empire. From what his wife says, the girls are only expected to marry well and perhaps bring their husbands to join the firm."

"A little antiquated, don't you think?" Caterina started loading the luncheon dishes into the dishwasher.

Margaret Mary watched her from the kitchen stool. She took a sip of wine from the glass in front of her. "So it makes what Beatrice is doing all the more admirable. Her sisters are still teenagers."

"I thought she was very impressive, really innovative. I'm sure the party will go well."

"Are you going to be Rafe's date?"

Caterina paused in her cleaning, wondering where this was going. She turned. "I've been invited to be his plus one. I don't really consider it a date."

"What are you going to wear?"

The conversation was getting more uncomfortable. "Haven't thought of it." Caterina sought to change the subject and hit on the perfect topic. "I forgot to tell you. Paolo Benigni's mother is in Careggi Hospital. She's having a cardiac stent put in tomorrow. I know you have known her for years. I'm sure she would appreciate a visit."

"Why did you not tell me before now?" She looked at her watch and stood up, pushing her empty wine glass toward Caterina. "I will go tonight. Marcella must be so bored waiting. Much better to see her now than after the procedure. Marcella Fontana-Benigni won't want anyone to visit when she is not looking her best."

CHAPTER FOURTEEN

By mid-morning on Monday, the report from the burglary division had arrived on Caterina's desk, detailing the crime scene findings from the theft at the French students' apartment, including fingerprint analysis that linked the incident to other similar occurrences. The most interesting part of the report, she thought, was a one-page analysis prepared by Detective Massimo Castagna, who had discovered that the same rental agency managed the apartment leases for all of the locations that had been looted.

Caterina summarized the findings of the file for the magistrate and calendared a reminder for herself to check with Castagna's superior to coordinate follow-up with the schools utilizing the rental agency's services.

Patricia Benvenuti, after letting her know that the magistrate would not be in until late in the day, told Caterina that the mayor's office was tentatively scheduling an event on Wednesday to honor the refugee for his bravery. The mayor's press secretary, Taddeo Toddi, wanted it to take place mid-week for maximum coverage by all available news outlets.

"Taddeo, I think Wednesday will work," Caterina said when she got him on the phone. "Given that there were no health complications over the weekend, he can stand and walk through the event, but his doctor says the bruising around his jaw and eye will not be gone." Toddi didn't think that would be a problem, so she added, "Would the mayor's office consider providing Mr. Nadja with housing for a couple of weeks, perhaps in a *pensione* or one of the monasteries? The friars at Ognissanti sometimes have extra rooms. They've been very supportive of the mayor's efforts to bring about a rational resolution to the problem of undocumented immigrants in Florence. Or perhaps since the nuns in Piazza Carmine actually rent rooms to families, they take in men and might have a space for Adamou."

Toddi said he would arrange for thirty days of housing and incorporate that information in Mayor Moretti's speech. Caterina offered to translate for Adamou Nadja during the press conference, but Toddi said they had another African, who spoke both French and Italian, "to increase the optics, you know."

"Taddeo, Adamou is not going to understand your 'optics.' He's a simple man just trying to take care of himself and improve his family's circumstances.

"Why don't we go to the hospital together and discuss all of this with him. I can use the mayor's car and driver this afternoon. I'll pick you up in an hour. That will give me some time to set up accommodations for the young man."

Caterina agreed, but added, "We are going to need Mr. Nadja to testify if charges are brought against the men who assaulted him."

"Sorry, Caterina. I believe the mayor has decided to concede that issue to Captain Ventroni, who decided not to arrest them. It muddies the good news message of refugee heroism if Florentine citizens are charged with beating up said hero. You get my meaning?"

"That's not right, Taddeo."

"It is what it is, Caterina. Forget it and move on. Be glad your young African is getting his residency visa and a chance at a new life."

"In a city that despises him and a country that turns her back on his kind."

"That's part of the reason for the press conference," he said. "We are trying to change hearts and minds."

Caterina's cell phone started ringing. "I've got to take another call, Taddeo. Let's talk tomorrow."

It was Rafe. "I'd like to note that it's still raining. I did my morning run in the rain and that part of the bank where we had our little adventure last Thursday is all underwater now."

"That happens once or twice every winter. It's just a little early this year," She said in rote fashion as she jotted a couple of notes about her call with the mayor's press secretary before focusing on Rafe.

"What can I do for you?"

"I just wanted you to know that everybody made it to the hotel yesterday, including Jake and Ross, so the party is going forward as planned. Do you want me to pick you up?"

"I've got a few more things to do this morning. When do we have to be at the Stibbert?"

"Remember Beatrice said the museum closes to the public at two and opens for the reception at four, meaning drinks on the terrace." He paused. "Or inside, I guess, if this damn rain doesn't stop. Then the museum is open for an hour, starting at five. So you have to be there by then because I lose my scavenger hunt expert if you're late."

"You go ahead at four. I'll be there in time. We'll both work on ordering up some sun, although these days in October it's setting around five. Remember it's good luck in Italy to have rain on a wedding day."

"They're already married. A wet party is just a wet party."

"Cheer up, Rafe. No matter what, it will be unforgettable."

Forty-five minutes later, Taddeo Toddi called from the mayor's car parked outside the Questura, "If you're ready, let's go now. The rain isn't going to clear and traffic will be slow."

As they wove through the streets out to the large hospital complex on the edge of the city, Caterina told him that she would be coming this way later for an event at the Museo Stibbert."

"Too bad you don't have your party clothes with you," said Taddeo. "We could have dropped you off on the way back from the hospital."

"I'll probably miss the *aperitivo* on the terrace – or more likely inside, given the weather – but I'll be in time for the scavenger hunt."

"*Cos'è una 'scavenger hunt'*?" Taddeo asked.

"It's like *una caccia al tesoro*, a hunt for treasure, a game. A bunch of Americans will be searching Stibbert's collection for certain items, hoping to be the team that will find the most."

"I was at the *museo* for Queen Elizabeth's birthday party, hosted by the British Consulate before they closed the consulate down. I guess that event won't be happening next year."

Caterina nodded. "I had a meeting with the unpaid volunteer, I guess the word is 'honorary,' Consul General, Dame Annabelle Berkshire, last month. She seems very serious about her job, so if she can find someone to sponsor the event, I bet the Queen's birthday will still be celebrated by the British expat community."

"I hope so. I'm very partial to Champagne with tiny sandwiches and those little cakes with marzipan icing," Taddeo said with a reminiscent smile. "That being said, any party at the Stibbert will be fun, even in the rain."

Adamou Nadja could see out of both eyes, although one lid was still swollen and and the eye was bloodshot.

The bandage on his nose had been replaced with a less bulky version. Taddeo Toddi wondered aloud if there was an option to switch it out for a darker colored tape or perhaps a Band-Aid.

Caterina looked at him with disapproval. "Optics, again?" she said in Italian, switching from French, which she was using with Adamou. Taddeo reddened and went off to find the nurse.

Caterina turned back to the patient and told him about the offer of the friars at the Ognissanti Monastery to provide him a room and meals for at least the next month.

"Perhaps they have some work I can do in exchange for their kindness," Adamou Nadja offered.

Caterina put her hand on his shoulder, saying, "Take it slow, Mr. Nadja. Wednesday is going to be very tiring and your ribs still need time to heal."

"But I cannot take advantage of such kindness."

"The brothers at Ognissanti are in the kindness business," she said with a smile. "I'm sure if they feel it is in your best interest, they will find you something to do, while still taking care of any physical limitations you have."

Later, as the mayor's driver pulled up outside her apartment building on the Lungarno Solderini, Taddeo Toddi assured Caterina that he would arrange for Adamou Nadja's transportation after his discharge from the hospital the next morning.

"Have a great time tonight," he said in parting. "Watch out for the ghost of Frederick Stibbert. I heard he haunts the halls wearing a suit of armor."

CHAPTER FIFTEEN

With ten minutes to spare, Caterina stepped out of a taxi at the gates of Museo Stibbert. The villa was lit from below by spotlights that caused the yellow plaster to glow and caught the myriad coats-of-arms and other stone carvings that graced the walls. Two dozen flaming torches cast dancing light over the terrace. The rain had stopped mid-afternoon so there were only a few puddles for the guests bedecked in party attire to avoid.

Caterina took a glass of Prosecco from a waiter dressed as a Renaissance page boy in a doublet of embroidered ruby velvet. She gave a mental nod to Beatrice's production skills.

Guests in colorful cocktail attire roamed the terrace, exploring the garden folly, a tiny domed building with a green and yellow ceramic roof. Inside was a life-size marble statue of a nude Venus. The more energetic took the stairway by torchlight down into the garden where Frederick Stibbert had constructed an Egyptian temple with two giant stone pharaohs guarding the door. The temple overlooked a man-made lake. Two swans paddled through the lily pads.

Instrumental arrangements of George Gershwin and Cole Porter played in the background. Caterina couldn't tell if they came from a recording or musicians inside the gallery that ran along the back of the terrace.

Her eyes were drawn through the crowd to two tall men standing at the low outer wall, overlooking the vast garden in the opposite direction from the temple and lake. One was dark and slender, the other blond and broad.

"Wow!" said Rafe. "You clean up nice."

Caterina glanced down at her aubergine crepe wrap dress that hugged her curves over high-heeled black Sergio Rossi boots that made her almost as tall as Rafe. Her hair was swept high in a French braid and black Venetian glass earrings dangled to her shoulders.

"Always the smooth talker, Mathews," jibed Max Turner with a laugh. He greeted Caterina with an easy brush of both cheeks in the Italian manner.

"Who's smooth? Look at you with your European moves, Turner." Above the collar of his black leather blazer, Rafe's color was high.

Caterina thought he couldn't decide between a handshake or a peck on the cheek. He took her arm instead and entwined it with his. Maybe as a sign to his old friend. She welcomed the moral support because this was the first time she had seen the Legal Attaché from the U.S. Embassy in Rome since the spring when she had harbored a major crush on him. Then she learned that he was married.

"Max, I hear you brought Julia and the kids with you," she said. "It's great to see you. It's been a while." Shut up, Caterina, she told herself, stop babbling.

Although Rafe lifted an eyebrow, Max didn't seem to notice anything amiss. "Julia stepped inside. She got a bit chilled, so she and Zandra headed in with the stated goal of finding the party planner."

"How do the grooms like the place you and Zandra selected for their celebration?" Caterina asked Rafe.

"They are over the moon," laughed Max, at the same time Rafe said, "I hardly had anything to do with the selection, but I'm glad to take any credit that comes my way. Both Ross and Jake are amazed at my newly acquired Italian taste in clothes and my previously unrecognized talent for inventive social gatherings. The clothes, they admit, sadly comes from the fact that I am scrawny enough to fit into shirts and jackets with a tapered line. The skill of throwing a grand party is only an illusion."

"Anyone could throw a fancy do at a house like this," Max said. "It's my first visit and I can't wait to come back with the kids. The house itself is a party."

"So why are you out here in the damp?" asked Caterina, taking a sip of her bubbly wine.

"Rafe and I were trying to solve a mystery in the garden down there." He waved an arm out over the trees and hedges on the steep sloping hill.

"Sounds interesting," said Caterina, glad of the change of subject, still holding Rafe's arm and turning with him to the view. "What's so mysterious about the garden?"

"About ten minutes ago, two guys were standing on the other side of that little lake down there," Rafe said. "It was too dim among the trees to get a good look at them, but they seemed to be having an argument."

"In both Italian and English," interjected Max. "A mix of both, it seemed."

"I swear, I knew one of them." Rafe let go of her arm and placed his hands on the wall, leaning forward, looking in the the darkening woods.

"What were they fighting about?" Caterina moved beside him. She couldn't see anyone in the part of the garden that sloped away to the street far below. No other building blacked the view.

Max answered, "We couldn't tell. But they saw us watching and moved off into the trees. Rafe thinks they were heading toward the exit to the garden way down the hill. See it there under the street light?" He pointed to a pair of tall wrought-iron gates that opened to the side street. "We were waiting to see if we could get a look at them as they left under the lights."

"Why so interested in two random guys?" she asked.

"If it was the man I thought I saw, he's bad news," Rafe said.

Caterina thought she saw a movement in the gloom. "It's probably my imagination…"

"*There!*" Rafe shouted, causing the people behind them on the terrace to turn.

Two dark figures moved quickly through the lighted opening and were gone down the narrow street.

"Max, I swear it was him."

"Impossible," said Max.

"Why?" asked Caterina.

"That man died in Syria three months ago."

CHAPTER SIXTEEN

Caterina rounded on the two American men, "What do you mean 'he's dead'?"

Max shook his head. "It's a long story. I don't even know if it's something we *can* tell you about."

"What do you mean?"

Max looked annoyed that he had to say more. "The mission was classified. It involved American security services."

Caterina persisted. "Are you talking FBI or CIA or NSA or military?

"A bit of all four," said Rafe with a look that told Caterina he wished that he had said nothing. "Caterina, don't interrogate Max. He can't talk about it."

"But…," Caterina started.

"Max and Rafe get your butts inside." It was Zandra, dressed in what could only be called, "a little black tux," without the frilly shirt, or any shirt at all. She hooked arms with the two men, urging them toward the museum entrance. "The scavenger hunt is going to start. Come on, Caterina. You and Rafe are paired with me and Jake. I'm hoping having a Florentine ringer on the team gives us the edge we need. Max, you and Julia are with Ross and his mother."

Caterina made a grab at Rafe's free arm. "Just one minute. You can't leave me with no explanation."

Rafe took her hand. "There's nothing to do about this now. I'll figure out how much I can tell you later. Now let's just enjoy the party. I plan to win this scavenger hunt."

Max's wife, Julia, was waiting at the door. Whatever Caterina had imagined about his wife when she worked with Max after the Easter bombing was dispelled in a moment. With a slender runner's physique, Julia Turner was petite, but she added height for the party with three-inch heels. She wore an off-shoulder, nipped-waist rose satin cocktail dress with a short flared skirt. Her golden hair was cut short and layered around her delicate features.

Her first words, "Max has told me all about you. I am happy to put a face to the stories!" so disconcerted Caterina that all she could say was, "What did you do with Josh and Maddy tonight?"

Julia laughed. "It's such a relief to get out of 'mom clothes' for an evening. The American Consul General – do you know Susan Whitmore? – has a teenage daughter.

So we dropped the kids at the Consulate on our way here and caught a lift with Susan."

Standing behind Julia were two men – Jake, young with military bearing, dressed in a simple dark suit and open-collared white shirt, and Ross, older, shorter, softer, in a plaid jacket, jacquard waistcoat, and a natty bow tie – and an elegant older woman, Ross's mother. By the time introductions were made they were at the end of the crowd of about three dozen party-goers streaming up the stairs into the museum.

"My mother said the ballroom was so interesting in its own right that with her arthritis, she's staying there," said Jake. "My father decided to remain with her as has Ross's Aunt Judy. Everyone else is taking part in the hunt. I think only you, Caterina, and Susan Whitmore have a hometown advantage."

They crossed a short, dark hallway, went through a tall door, and emerged into a ornate room with a high ceiling lit by a huge crystal chandelier. The walls were covered in patterned maroon brocade, which was in turn covered by dozens of portraits of 16th century Florentine nobility. Suits of armor stood along one side, drawing much attention from the military members of the party. A giant malachite table stood in the center of the room under the chandelier.

Beatrice Forzoni stood in front of the grand fireplace and called for quiet. "This is known as the Malachite Room and it is where you will start your scavenger hunt. My assistant is passing out the lists of items or decorative features you must find. All you need to do is snap a photograph to memorialize your find. Be advised that no list is exactly identical to any other, so it won't help to follow each other around, watching how your friends are progressing."

She pointed out a young man, dressed in a doublet with a soft cap sporting a long feather. "In each room there will be a helper. Most of them are guides in the museum during the day and are quite knowledgeable. Some of them speak English. Others, however, know little about the museum and speak only Italian."

"You need to be fairly efficient in your search if you are serious about winning a prize. You only have one hour to get through the museum, which has over fifty rooms and more than ten thousand items on display."

Caterina and Zandra looked at the list the helper handed to Rafe. Their list read:

Medici children with nurse

Embossed leather wallpaper

Scimitar with gold and ebony grip

Stibbert's own doors

St. George and the dragon

Tired knight

Young Japanese warrior

Mother's lion

First toilet

Emperor's new clothes

"Piece of cake," Caterina said. "At least for half of the list."

Zandra warned, "We have some competition across the room. Rob and George have been vacationing in Florence for the past ten years. They know this museum. Rob has a thing about armor and George has never met an antique chair he didn't want to own."

Max overheard her as he was scanning the list in Julia's hand. "Don't forget the Consul General. She's already moving her group to the next room, saying something about 'a Murano glass chandelier shedding light on a nude' – whatever that means."

"Who's our photographer?" asked Caterina. When Jake raised a hand holding an iPhone, she pointed at a large portrait hanging high on the wall above a tapestry. "That's a painting of two of the Medici daughters – maybe those of Lorenzo the Magnificent, I can't remember – and their nurse, the old woman in black."

"One down, nine to go," Jake said as he snapped a photo.

"I'm not sure what a scimitar is," said Caterina, crossing out the first item with a small pen from her clutch purse.

"A curved sword frequently found in Arab countries," said Rafe. "Not used so much any more in the age of automatic weapons and IEDs."

"So it'll be in the Islamic Room," said Caterina, leading the way. "It's close by."

They entered a room so completely different from the European elegance of the first two rooms that it rendered the group speechless for a moment. Then Jake whistled. "This guy sure was hooked on the military regalia."

The hall contained a short parade of Arab soldier mannequins in chain mail and silks riding full-size plaster horses. The walls were lined with centuries old weapons.

"Check out that ceiling," said Zandra. Then she pointed, "Are those scimitars, Rafe?"

"More than two dozen," said Jake. "We need to find the one with a gold and ebony grip." He edged past one of Bea's helpers dressed as a Bedouin princess. "Here it is." He took the shot and then another of the girl. "I've got to get more photos in each room. I'll never remember all this later."

Zandra cautioned, "Then make sure you 'heart' the ones for the scavenger hunt."

"What do you mean?"

Zandra took his phone and showed him the place to mark the competition photos, then urged him on to the next room.

The embossed leather wallpaper was in one of the parlors. Jake took a close-up shot while Zandra exclaimed over the collection of snuff boxes. Ross was across the room, pointing at a large Qing Dynasty porcelain vase that was apparently on their scavenger hunt list. He turned to his groom, saying, "Honey, I am getting so many ideas for our weekend place. What did you think of the crown molding in the last room?"

Jake groaned, "I'm not even sure what a crown molding is, but I did appreciate how this Stibbert fellow displayed his collection of dueling pistols in the last corridor." He winked at Zandra. "What do you think about the Knights Templar shield as a design choice?"

She waved him off. "I'm not getting between the two of you, especially on the subject of décor. You know I'm a minimalist at heart, white on white. I'm getting a bit claustrophobic here."

While the others were distracted, Caterina pulled Rafe to one side. "It's driving me crazy not knowing anything about this guy who is 'bad news' and 'dead'," she said, making air quotes with her fingers. "Tell me *something*, anything."

"His identity is not classified, and his name would mean nothing to you."

"What did he do?"

"He was an arms dealer to, among others, ISIS."

Sensing they were drawing looks from Zandra and Jake, she called out, "The doors that Stibbert painted are in the next room or the one after. Look at the back side of each door. One has a sun on it and the other, a moon. Make sure Ross sees them. He may want to add a bit of *trompe l'oeil* in your weekend place, Jake." He moaned and Zandra made a show of pushing him through the next doorway.

She and Rafe walked slowly behind the other two. "And how did you know him?" she asked.

"He was the reason I was locked in a cellar in Homs," Rafe muttered.

She stopped and pulled him around, staring into his face. "The place Jake and his team got you out of?"

Rafe nodded.

"So how did he die?"

"That's what's classified. I can't tell you anything about that."

Caterina took another tack. "What's he doing in Florence?"

"The better question is what is he doing alive?"

CHAPTER SEVENTEEN

Zandra, who had wandered on ahead with Jake, came rushing back. She grabbed both Rafe and Caterina by their arms, urging them on, saying, "Hurry up you two. It's the most amazing room of dozens of Japanese samurai warriors and horses decked out in exotic armor. How did a guy living over a hundred years ago, without the internet, know about ancient Japanese military gear?"

Rafe and Caterina looked at each other, took a beat, and then burst out laughing.

"Ever heard of books, Zandra? Or explorers, who centuries ago were traveling the seas? By the time Stibbert was born, England was colonizing the world," said Rafe.

"Remember Bea told us that Stibbert's grandfather made a fortune in India in the mid-1800s."

Bea, dressed in a black A-line Prada dress, accessorized with a golden Japanese silk scarf and matching enamel earrings, was coming out of the gallery as they entered. She overheard their conversation and explained further, "Frederick Stibbert made it his business to know about ancient armor from every part of the world, but he had a special love for exotic Asian garb. You can imagine that such a flamboyant man, living in Victorian times – once he even showed Queen Victoria his collection – would want as much of the exquisite Japanese armor as he could find. He was well known among private collectors and museum curators. Auction houses and agents were constantly bringing items to his notice, hoping he would make more and more expensive purchases."

Rafe and Caterina joined the others in the grand room with its highly decorated dark wood ceiling. Plaster models of samurai soldiers marched across the floor, arrayed in colorful armor of wood, iron, cloth, and leather. Hundreds of samurai swords, sheathed in metal, carved ivory, or painted wood were presented in glass cases, as were elaborate decorated helmets.

"Burt's giving a tutorial on samurai military dress," said Jake, pointing at a beefy guy with a shaved head. "Where did he learn words like *kasuri*, *mengu*, and *jingosa*, much less knowing that it's lacquer that gives the metal those vibrant colors."

"Remember?" said Zandra. "He was stationed in Okinawa two years ago. He's got his own sword collection that he keeps trying to impress the girls with. Not that it does him much good. My husband tried to suggest that Burt might want to try the more traditional dinner and a movie route, but Burt hasn't caught on, yet. I wish Patrick could see this place. Once he sees Jake's photos he's going to regret thinking his law firm's annual retreat was more important than a great party in Tuscany." She asked Jake to take photos of the series of paintings depicting European medieval costumes lining the wall high above the glass cases filled with Japanese armor, a strange, but pleasingly colorful, juxtaposition of two cultures.

Rafe pointed at a pint-sized uniformed mannequin with a helmet, holding a spear. "Is that the 'young Japanese warrior' from our list?" He turned to his teammate. "Snap that photo, Jake. We're not here for the learning. We're in it to win."

Caterina waited for Jake to finish fumbling with his iPhone before saying, "If you want to see something truly incredible, we should get to the Hall of the Cavalcade."

If the Americans had thought the contents of the villa were over the top, *La Sala della Cavalcata*, as Caterina told them the name in Italian, rendered them speechless, until Zandra gasped, "Holy moly, this Stibbert guy takes hoarding to a whole new level."

Below the balcony where they were standing was the biggest hall by far. The ceiling was three stories high and down the center of the gallery were six or seven rows of horses, two abreast, dressed in full equine armor with knights similarly clad in battle dress from the 16th and 17th centuries. If this was not enough, the walls were lined with full or partial suits of armor and glass cases of swords, pikes, helmets, and shields. The hall was in evocative shadows, lit by small spotlights from the corners.

"The villa doesn't look that big from the outside," Rafe said.

"Last year, one of the guides told the group I was with that Frederick Stibbert bought the next-door villa and joined them together. You really can't get a sense of the scale unless you walk around the whole complex," Caterina said. "It was when he made that purchase that he started thinking that his collection had the makings of a museum."

Zandra poked Rafe in the ribs. "It was probably after his mother started complaining that he had too much stuff." She turned to Caterina and asked, "You did say his mother lived with him, didn't you?"

Caterina nodded. "But she was a strange one, too. Wait until you see the frescos in her bedroom. Remember the 'mother's lion' we need to find? It was the last thing she saw before closing her eyes each night."

"There must have been some fine parties in this place," said Jake as he took photos of the cavalcade. "Bea told Ross that Stibbert entertained Oscar Wilde and Lord Alfred Douglas back in the day. Can you just imagine how Wilde described this place in his letters? Too bad he didn't set a play in Florence. Frederick would have made a great character."

Rafe directed his attention to the far end of the hall. "Look up on that ledge! I think it's St. George slaying a dragon."

"I wonder what Mamma Stibbert said when he brought home a life-sized sculpture with a dragon," mused Zandra.

Caterina laughed. "She probably thought it fit fine in this space rather than in her living quarters. Let's go downstairs and find the 'tired knight' – it's a wooden carving clad in miniature armor, if I remember right – who is sitting in one of the corners. Then we should head on to the bedrooms and the ballroom."

"Maybe one of Bea's 'helpers' can assist us," said Rafe. "I saw two of them dressed as knights among the cavalcade. I bet they're sweating in all that metal. Bea certainly came through with the fun realistic touches. I remember she said Frederick used to like to play dress-up with his collection."

They were still talking about the Roman coliseum, complete with a lion and a gladiator, depicted in a mural around Mrs. Stibbert's elegant bed and the fact that Frederick owned Napoleon's coronation robes from when he was crowned Emperor of Italy, when they took the stairs down from the musicians' balcony, where a string quartet played, into the ballroom below. The grand carpet had been rolled up to expose the intricate parquet wood floor. Five tables, set with fine china and crystal for eight, glowed with tall tapered candles. Ross and Jake shared a long table in front of the high carved wood fireplace with their parents and the two witnesses from their wedding, Zandra and Burt.

Caterina sat between Rafe and Max, but spent most of her time speaking across Rafe to Julia Turner about the joys and trials of bringing up two children under the age of six in Rome. Rafe finally offered to switch seats with her between the appetizer course of tiny crostini and the service of pasta with porcini mushrooms. Julia started a subtle interrogation about Caterina's intentions regarding Rafe. Caterina quickly turned that to an inquiry about Rafe's background.

"So did you meet Rafe when he and Max were at Quantico?"

Julia nodded, but then said, "They met there in a class, but, of course, they weren't training together."

"But I thought they came up through the FBI at the same time and posted as Legal Attachés to different embassies. When I worked with Max last spring, Rafe was in Lebanon."

"He may have been in Lebanon, but he wasn't a Legal Attaché. Rafe isn't with the FBI."

"Then what? Is he with the State Department?"

Without either of them noticing, Max had come to stand behind his wife. He leaned down, saying, "Sweetheart, can you help Zandra with something? I think it has to do with the cake." He led her away from the table.

Caterina turned to Rafe. "Are you working with the FBI or not?"

He hesitated while the waiter took their pasta bowls away. "Well, since that time in Homs, I'm sorta on sabbatical. You know I was a mess afterwards. I'd dropped twenty pounds and they had worked me over, if you know what I mean."

"I remember what you were like when you got here in July, but what I want to know is when you went back to

Washington in early September were you debriefed by the FBI or some other agency?" Caterina immediately saw the escape hatch her question gave him.

"I think you can probably say that the whole alphabet of agencies got a crack at me," he said with a chuckle. "Thus, the need for the sabbatical," he tried to joke as the waiters served the main course of scampi and baby vegetables,.

"You're not going to tell me."

He took a sip from his glass of wine. "Tell you what?"

"Rafe, when you met Max at Quantico, he was training for the FBI. Were you with the CIA?

"The CIA doesn't train at Quantico."

She frowned as she speared a tiny carrot. "That's not an answer to my question. Who is your…"

"Let's talk about this tomorrow. This food is just too good not to give it our full attention."

Caterina let him have his way, but ate in silence until the plates were cleared and a small goat cheese salad was served. Rafe was soon caught up in a conversation with a member of the Seal Team about a new app that the squad was using on long distance runs to track health and fitness statistics.

The clink of a spoon against a crystal goblet ushered in the toasts. Zandra gave the first salute to the guests of honor, followed by jokes from Burt, well wishes from the parents, and finally, speeches by Jake and Ross. The champagne flowed and the cheers got louder with every toast.

The chandeliers in the room dimmed as a towering cake bedecked with hundreds of tiny candles was rolled past the doors of the ballroom, down the adjoining gallery to the Peacock Room. From the musician's balcony, two trumpeters in Renaissance garb played a fanfare.

The attendees broke into applause. Beatrice, who had throughout the dinner discreetly directed the table service, now announced that the party would gather in the gallery for the cutting of the cake.

"One of Frederick Stibbert's ceremonial sabers will be used to cut the first two pieces," she said. "And after the cake is served, I will announce the winners of the scavenger hunt."

Max and Julia came up behind Rafe and Caterina in the hall. They had their coats on.

"We've got to get back to the Consulate. We promised the babysitter that we wouldn't be late. She has school tomorrow," Julia explained. "The party planner called us a taxi."

"Wish the guys all the best," said Max. "They sure had a memorable party."

Julia added, "I sure hope you two will come to Rome for a visit. We've got a guest room, but we can always vacate the kids' room, if you don't want to share.

Caterina couldn't meet Rafe's eyes, but heard his choked laughter. She gave Julia a quick hug, brushing both cheeks, doing the same with Max before he took his wife's hand and pulled her out the open tall glass French doors off the gallery onto the terrace.

Applause went up as the cake was sliced, followed by a scream echoing through the halls of the museum.

CHAPTER EIGHTEEN

Jake and his ten Seal Team brothers were the first down the corridor, followed by Rafe and Caterina. Cries for help followed the initial scream, but it was hard for Caterina to tell from where they came.

"It's got to be on this level," said Beatrice, coming up from behind. "We could not hear a cry from the upper floors, the walls are too thick. And it's not as close as the musicians' balcony."

The men split off taking different corridors and stairs.

"Who is left in the museum?" Caterina asked Bea.

"My helpers, at least those who are also employed by the museum, are supposed to be closing and locking the rooms, but they should be done by now. I sent the senior guide Katia Ponti through to make sure everything was done properly."

"Where would Katia's last stop be?" asked Rafe.

"Perhaps *La Sala della Cavalcata*."

"Take us there."

Rafe and Caterina followed Bea until they were running down the four stone steps into the hall with the cavalcade of armored horses and riders. In the far corner, under the ledge where St. George was killing his dragon, a woman dressed in black slacks and a sweater was standing over a fallen knight in armor. "Hurry!" she cried. "Help him."

At first it appeared as if one of the plaster mannequins had fallen off its horse or been dislodged from its post along the wall, but the metal suit was of lightweight shiny aluminum and a pool of blood spread around the shoulders. The hilt and part of a narrow blade protruded from the breastplate at an angle up into the chest.

"Emilio!" screamed Bea, dropping to her knees beside his head.

"Let's get his helmet off," said Rafe crouching beside her. "Maybe he's just injured. Help me, Caterina. Don't touch the weapon until we know what we're dealing with. Support his neck."

Caterina slid her hands under each side of where the helmet met the shoulder plates. As Rafe eased the helmet off, Caterina saw a young pugilist's face with a muscular neck adorned with black tattoos as she eased the man's head to the floor. She checked for a carotid pulse, but found none. His skin was cold. Rafe confirmed her finding. He shook his head.

"He's gone. It's been a while." He moved aside as Bea came closer, looking down at the prone figure.

"*Mio Dio, chi è?*" Bea exclaimed. "Who is he?" she repeated. "That's not Emilio Esposito."

Jake came running up just as Katia caught sight of the dead man's face and fainted. Jake caught her, half kneeling as he lowered her to the floor.

"Is he dead?" Jake asked.

Rafe nodded as Burt and Zandra joined the circle around the victim and woman on the terracotta floor.

"I see the knife in him," said Burt, "but what happened to her?" He peered down at the woman in Jake's arms.

Zandra reached down to pull out the knife.

"Don't touch that!" Caterina exclaimed.

"Oh my god, I'm sorry." Zandra backed up. "I wasn't thinking."

"Does someone have a phone?" asked Caterina. "I left mine at the table."

Bea pulled one out of the side pocket of her flared skirt. Jake found his and shifting Katia to his other arm, held it up.

"Call 113, Bea. Ask for the police and an ambulance," Caterina said as she turned to Jake. "Let me have yours." She dialed Magistrate Benigni's home number from memory.

When her boss answered, she said in Italian, "Sir, I have a situation at Museo Stibbert. A probable homicide. It is going to need someone of Dr. Rosselli's caliber to investigate the crime scene." She scanned the grand hall with its dark shadows, hundreds of ancient weapons and suits of armor, and dozens of places to hide. "It will be very complex from an evidentiary point of view and even more complicated because there were about fifty Americans in the villa when the victim was killed. Not that they are among the suspects, but they will have to be interviewed. The police have been called. Could you arrange it with Dr. Rosselli?"

The magistrate only asked a couple of questions and rang off after requesting that Caterina call him with more details as soon as possible.

"Dr. Rosselli is the director of the Crime Scene Investigative Unit," Caterina explained to Rafe as she handed the phone back to Jake. Then she said, "Rafe, please call Max and ask him to come back here as soon as he can. As Legal Attaché to the Embassy in Rome, he needs to follow the investigation and assist with the witness statements from the party guests. Given Ross's job with a member of congress, there is the potential of press coverage. If the victim turns out not to be Italian, it's going to be even more complicated." She paused for a minute, looking down at the dead man, and then back up at Rafe's face. "You don't know him, do you?"

Rafe looked confused, switching his gaze from the man to Caterina, back to the man, and then back to her. Finally, his face cleared. "No, it's not him."

She lowered her voice to be heard by him alone. "Not the mysterious 'supposed to be dead' man you thought you saw tonight?"

"Not even close. This guy is at least ten years younger and looks like a punk kid rather than an international arms dealer."

"I'm not sure what one of those would look like," she murmured before turning to Bea, Zandra and Burt. She asked Bea to make sure her staff didn't leave the premises until the police had come and interviewed them. "Then please go out and meet the police who arrive and bring them back here."

She asked Burt and Zandra to gather all of the guests in the ballroom. "If you can find some paper, have everybody write their name, cell phone number, email address and and the name of the hotel where they are staying. That may make things go faster, although I'm not guaranteeing it."

Finally, she looked down at Jake, who was still holding the unconscious Katia Ponti. "Is she coming around?"

"Not yet, but I think it's just a faint. She's breathing fine. Maybe the emergency folks will have an ammonia inhalant to bring her around. I'll carry her down to the other end, so she won't see him when she wakes. Do you think she knows him?"

"I have no idea, but she's the closest thing we have to a witness at this point. Don't take her too far until the medical team checks her out." Just as she turned to Rafe, the rest of the Seal Team, which had been searching the villa, arrived on the balcony over the great hall. "Hey, you men stay there. We've got a crime scene down here and don't need anyone else in it," she called.

She turned back to Rafe, "Can you get them to stand guard at each door to this space and keep everyone out. Even the police. I don't want anyone in here until Dr. Rosselli arrives with his team. Don't worry, I'll deal with the officers who turn up. Just hold the doors. I'm staying here until then."

As Jake picked up Katia and turned to follow Rafe, he looked over his shoulder, "Didn't Mathews tell me that you worked on a case a few months ago — something about a murder in a museum? Even in a city full of museums, this seems to be a bit too much of a coincidence."

CHAPTER NINETEEN

With gratitude, Caterina accepted a second espresso from Patricia Benvenuti the next morning. She was exhausted from the long night and there was an unpleasant void left when the adrenalin wore off.

"Dr. Rosselli took the body to the coroner at about midnight. We let the party guests leave just before then. Most of them are at the Hotel Regency in Piazza D'Azeglio and will be there through tomorrow and some, even longer." She was in the magistrate's office briefing her boss and making a plan for any follow-up. "Captain Gentile from the Montughi *Commissariato* has charge of the investigation. Max and I translated for him during the group interview to move things along. Most everyone on the scavenger hunt noticed at least one of the three helpers wearing armor in the Hall of the Cavalcade, but those who tried to get information out of any one of them found that none of them spoke English so the interactions were short, if at all."

"Were there three or four costumed knights?" Paolo Benigni asked, thumbing through her report. "I couldn't determine from what is here."

"Four men, but only three costumes." She flipped through her copy. "Look on page four. Emilio Esposito left early. He took off his costume in the cantina where all of the guides, waiters, musicians, and helpers changed during the evening. He didn't know who used the armor after he left. Nobody was in the cantina when he took off the costume."

"Was his departure planned?"

"He says he told Beatrice Forzoni, the event planner, that he couldn't stay past six. She says she didn't remember him telling her this, but that it wouldn't have mattered since the scavenger hunt was done by then. She used some of the other costumed helpers during dinner, but just wanted two wearing armor at the door nearest to the ballroom to stop any guests from wandering back into the museum. She thought Emilio was one of the two, but she admits that she didn't check on this."

"What about the other personnel who were actually in the museum during the dinner?"

"From what Bea told Captain Gentile, the closure of the museum is a complex process requiring that each room and cabinet be checked and locked. Katia Ponti was in charge of a team of three guides and they methodically went through the museum together. They didn't see anyone else as they made their rounds. The three assistants were finishing up in the large Japanese gallery when Katia went on to the Hall of the Cavalcade. She found the body almost immediately and raised the alarm. She says nobody else was in the hall as far as she could tell, but of course you know what it is like in that part of the museum. It would be easy to hide and slip away unnoticed."

The magistrate closed the report, steepled his hands under his chin, and asked, "What did Dr. Rosselli say about time and mode of death?"

"He estimated that the man was killed between seven and nine, but Katia screamed at nine fifteen, and the body was cold to the touch at that time, so I would posit that the earlier end of Dr. Rosselli's time frame is more likely. Emilio's costume was available at six, so…"

The magistrate spoke as she hesitated, "He was stabbed. What kind of knife was it?"

"The murder weapon was an antique dirk, made of iron, sharp, narrow, a type of dagger, and most likely from the Stibbert collection. There is a photograph of it on the last page of the report."

"That means it could have been a planned killing or one of opportunity or passion."

"I suppose. We'll know more about the weapon when the museum employee who curates the weapons collection gets to examine it this morning. And, of course, we will have a better idea of the motive once we learn who the victim is."

"There was no identification on the body?"

Caterina shook her head. "And none in the cantina. He was wearing spandex shorts and shirt – the kind that bicyclists wear. Captain Gentile is having his team canvass the neighborhood looking for a bicycle or a scooter or a car."

"What kind of shoes was he wearing?"

"Good question." Caterina laughed. "That was the only thing he left in the cantina – a pair of Nike running shoes. He was wearing the leather costume shoes that went with the suit of armor."

"Fingerprints on file?"

"No."

"So what is the next step? I don't see that our team has any role except to help with any further interviews of the American guests."

"Unless the victim turns out to be a foreigner."

"Unlikely, don't you think?"

"Very unlikely," Caterina answered, mentally closing the file on what would surely be an interesting case, but for someone else, not her. "Bernardo Gentile seems to be a very competent officer. Dr. Rosselli did a very thorough job investigating the crime scene."

"So what is your next step?" he repeated.

"I'm going to call Lt. Lombardi, Captain Gentile's second-in-command and ask if he needs any more information from the guests. I'll also ask him to keep me informed on their progress with the investigation."

The magistrate nodded and slipped her report into his desk drawer. "Keep Max Turner in the loop. The American Ambassador in Rome has already called to express Congresswoman McAllen's wishes that we make this as easy as possible for her chief of staff and his husband. She doesn't want an unrelated homicide to ruin their honeymoon."

"I will do that, Sir. I have a meeting scheduled with Mr. Turner this afternoon."

"Now, what about our refugee problem?"

Caterina flipped to a previous page in her notebook. "The mayor wants to have the press conference and ceremony honoring Adamou Nadja tomorrow. Taddeo Toddi and I met with Adamou yesterday. He is still very uncomfortable, but will be able to participate tomorrow. I think he was released this morning." Caterina stopped, a look of concern darkened her eyes. "*Mio Dio*, Sir, I forgot to ask how your mother is. Did she have the procedure?"

"Do not worry about it, Caterina. She's doing just fine, as if nothing had happened. Thank your mother for her visit on Sunday. Mother found it very diverting. I'm sure they will be planning a lunch together soon." He returned to the original subject. "You are, right, Mr. Nadja was discharged from the hospital this morning. Patricia gave me a note that said that the mayor arranged for the Ognissanti Monastery to take him in. One of the friars speaks French and the French Consulate is right across the piazza from the church. Maybe the mayor can use his persuasive powers to get the French to offer him residency in France. I'm sure he would be happier there."

An hour later, Caterina met Max Turner in the garden courtyard of the Hotel Regency. It was empty because the rain had just stopped. Caterina draped her raincoat over a wrought iron chair and Max wiped down another with his handkerchief.

"Julia and the children went back to Rome this morning," he informed her. "Jake and Ross are on their way to Sorrento, hopefully to have a less eventful – and sunnier – honeymoon."

"Did any of the guests have morning-after recollections that might help us with the investigation?"

Max shook his head. "But I asked them to send me digital files of all of the photos taken during the scavenger hunt and the dinner. I'll have my assistant sort through them for images of the Hall of the Cavalcade and any with Bea's staff dressed in armor."

"That's going to be a lot of photos."

"True, but I want to give Captain Gentile any help that I can and there doesn't seem to be much else I can do." He flipped through her report on the early investigation. "Did they locate Emilio Esposito?"

Caterina took a sip from a cooling cup of cappuccino on the low table between them. "He left the event early – just after the end of the scavenger hunt – and swears that he told Beatrice he was going. She claims that she knew nothing of the plan. She hired the staff for the full evening. They both agree that there was no other helper or guide scheduled to come in after the guests vacated the museum space and the dinner began."

"Have you been able to identify the victim?" he asked.

"Not by fingerprints and I wouldn't count on a DNA match. Captain Gentile says if nothing turns up today, a sketch will be put in the papers tomorrow."

A light rain started to fall. Max got up, folding the report and sticking it in the pocket of his suit jacket. "I don't expect you will need me further, so I'm planning to catch a train to Rome in the next hour or two."

Caterina put on her raincoat as she followed him out of the courtyard. "There is something else you might help me with, Max," she said as he held the door to the lobby for her. "It's about Rafe and the man he thinks he saw."

"You should talk to him directly about that," Max said, checking his watch.

"I'm not convinced he'll tell me the truth or give me the full story."

Max raised an eyebrow. "And what makes you think I will?"

"Because we've worked together before," she said as she took his arm and urged him off the lobby into the small library furnished in Italian Art-Deco style. "You know I would never jeopardize a high security operation or Rafe. I know you have your friend's best interests at heart."

He closed the door and leaned back against it. "What do you want to know?"

"Is Rafe working for the CIA?"

"Why do you think that he might be?"

"Unlike you, he wasn't the Legat at the Embassy in Lebanon this past April when we called him for background info on our case."

"How do you know that?"

"I googled it. It's amazing what the embassy sites can tell you. He held the position of political analyst. The Legat is always an FBI agent. An analyst can be anyone." She held up a hand as he started to speak. "And also how does an analyst go from the embassy in Beirut to a cellar in Homs, and why?"

"You need to talk to Rafe. I am sure he will tell you."

"Okay, but *you* tell me who is the man he thinks he saw. The arms dealer that should be dead."

"His name was Adrian Rook. All I know is that he was some sort of go-between brokering arms shipments between the Calabrian 'Ndràngheta clans and ISIS."

"Why would the mafia sell guns to ISIS?"

"Not just guns," Max said, his tone clipped, "but also, explosives, grenades, land mines and the occasional missile launcher. Pretty much anything that the Italian military stores in warehouses throughout the country. For money, of course." He paused, then added, "And for protection."

"Protection?"

"Have you ever wondered why there has never been an Islamic terrorist strike in Italy? Belgium, France, England, Spain and Germany have all been hit, but not Italy."

"That's absurd, Max." Trying to comprehend his theory, she asked, "You're saying that the 'Ndràngheta are *protecting* Italy?"

"Along with the other clans in Sicily and the north."

"Absurd," she repeated. "Like they have an agreement – 'we'll only sell you arms if you leave us alone' – to protect the motherland?"

Max nodded. "Kind of like the Sicilian mob letting the Americans land in Sicily during WWII. It's not the first time the families have played on the international stage."

"I certainly don't know as much about such things as you and your security services do, but I would argue that maybe Italy just has a longer history of fighting homegrown terrorists, so it manages to keep track of the potential threats better than some other countries."

"Maybe, but that seems to be an impossible task if you accept the widely held theory that the perpetrators are getting into Europe by hiding in the masses of refugees. Italy gets over eighty percent of all of the unauthorized arrivals from North Africa and the Middle East. Something or someone is protecting Italy."

"I'd love to debate this with you, but we're straying from the subject, Max," she said with a humorless laugh. "Why do you think Adrian Rook is dead?"

"Because Jake's Seal Team blew up his house in Homs."

"If he didn't die there, why come to Florence?"

"Hell if I know."

CHAPTER TWENTY

Within twenty-four hours, Captain Bernardo Gentile's patrol officers found the car used by the victim of the Museo Stibbert homicide. When they ran the license plates of all of the cars parked on Via di Montughi through the database, the owner of a silver Fiat sedan, parked about 100 feet up the hill from the museum, was found to be Leone Mollica, who lived in the San Frediano district on the other side of the Arno.

"When we contacted Mollica, he said his nephew Timo used the car on a regular basis and had not come home Monday night," Captain Gentile told the assembled crowd as he paced at the head of the conference room table. Officers from both the centralized burglary and homicide departments, as well as from the local Montughi neighborhood precinct sat around the table. Caterina took notes at her seat against the wall near the back of the room. "He identified a photograph of the victim as being Timo Monti, age nineteen, from Perugia. Timo was his sister's son, who after getting into trouble at home was sent to live in Florence just over two years ago. Mollica said something about hoping that by putting him into a private school in Florence where the friars would whip him into shape, it would fix his behavior problems at home."

Captain Gentile pinned a photograph of Timo in a school uniform to a large rolling bulletin board and on a large white board placed next to the cork board he wrote the victim's name. Studying the photo, Caterina thought that the friars had certainly failed since the broken nose and tattoos had been acquired sometime after the school photo was taken. She almost missed what the captain said next.

"We opened the trunk of the car and found a shopping bag containing a gold goblet, circa 1500, a set of dueling pistols in a wooden box and a dagger with a jewel encrusted handle." As he listed each item, he tacked up evidence photographs with measuring sticks showing the size of each piece.

The bag, emblazoned with the Gucci logo, was a meter long, but only half as high. The goblet was only eighteen centimeters from base to rim, about the width of a man's spread hand. The case for the pistols would have taken up most of the length of the bag. The dagger's hilt was short and thick, studded with rubies and emeralds, and steel blade was long, honed to a deadly point. It came with a leather sheath.

An officer from the burglary and theft division spoke up, "A representative from the Museo Stibbert has confirmed our suspicion that these items are from the collection."

"So is this a theft gone awry?" asked a homicide detective.

Captain Gentile seemed not to want to take a position. "The trouble Timo Monti got into in Perugia had to do with the theft of money and jewelry from a family friend. His uncle told me that the families settled the matter privately without involving the authorities, which is why we didn't have a record of Monti's fingerprints in the system."

"If this is a case of theft from the museum, why was he killed and why was he wearing armor?" The question came from Magistrate Primo Zaccheri who would be overseeing the case for prosecution if a culprit was found.

"We are operating on the theory that there was an accomplice and that perhaps there was a falling out between thieves," answered Captain Gentile. "But it is too early in our investigation to settle on any one hypothesis."

Magistrate Zaccheri didn't seem convinced. "Why did the accomplice leave the items in the car?"

"Perhaps the murder was discovered sooner than expected," offered one of the officers from the local precinct. "And we impounded the car quickly. There was no way to come back into the neighborhood with all of us there."

The man from the burglary and theft division, speculated, "Or maybe the accomplice has other items. We asked the museum to undertake an inventory. Of course, with thousands of items on display that will take a while."

"Were there any prints on the murder weapon?" asked the magistrate. Caterina stopped taking notes to listen. Here, after all of the speculation, was a factual issue, something that could actually lead to an arrest.

"None, except for the victim's own. It seems he may have tried to grab it before he died." Caterina sat back, mentally packing her briefcase and heading to the mayor's press conference.

Magistrate Zaccheri caught her attention again when he asked, "Did Dr. Rosselli make any determination from the angle of the wound whether the perpetrator was tall or short, male or female?"

Captain Gentile shook his head. "He refused to speculate since the knife came in low to pass below the breastplate of the armor. It could have been a short man stabbing straight in and up to the heart or a tall man angling up from below. I suppose a woman could do it, but that seems unlikely."

"Or maybe it was a suicide," said a young patrol man, *sotto voce*, as he leaned against the back wall near Caterina's seat. "Like the Japanese do it."

Not quiet enough though, since he was heard by Lt. Lombardi. "Don't be an idiot, Bartoli. Who would dress up like a knight to kill himself?"

Captain Gentile, who had been pinning up the crime scene photos, turned and glared at his underling. With just a jerk of his head, he sent Bartoli out of the room. The rest of the meeting consisted of listing the action items to be taken by each division to further the investigation.

As she was leaving the precinct station one of the detectives from the burglary division caught up with Caterina. "You are working that apartment theft case, aren't you? The one with the cute French girls."

"The apartment on Via Taddea, you mean?" She continued walking.

"Yeah. I'm Massimo Castagna. I caught the case and had the new guy in the office go through hours of CCTV footage from the camera at the corner of Via Taddea and Via Panicale. We think one of the perps was wearing striped high-top tennis shoes."

"Striped?" It seemed absurd to Caterina that this was the detail that had caught someone's attention.

The detective didn't appear to notice her skepticism. "Yeah. Impossible to tell the color on the footage, but maybe red and white. It's not much, but it's something."

"Why do you think he is my thief?"

"Black slacks, black hoody, black t-shirt, but the hood was off his head and his scarf, which wasn't black, was showing."

"So I'm guessing he's Italian."

"Of course," the detective laughed. "Italian mothers are always telling their kids not to go out without a scarf to keep their necks warm."

Caterina still argued, "Half the kids hanging out at the food hall in the *Mercato Centrale* are dressed that way. What made you suspect him?"

"Maybe it was the Hello Kitty backpack he had slung over one shoulder. Did *la bella ragazza francese bionda* tell you that the thief took her book bag?"

"No, she didn't," Caterina said with a laugh. "But if the hood was down, you must have a shot of his face."

"Nope. He had a baseball cap on." He left her at her Vespa and turned to go to his car. "We'll keep an eye out for those Converse high-tops for you."

CHAPTER TWENTY-ONE

The mayor's stocky press secretary stretched up to murmur in Caterina's ear. "The boss wanted to do this in the *Sala dei Cinquecento*, but he was worried that the crowd would be dwarfed by the room. So we are using the smaller *Sala dei Duecento*."

The Hall of the Two Hundred was certainly full enough, standing room only. The tapestries created half a century before by Bronzino and Pontormo contrasted with the modern seating of the Citizen Council of the city. Along the back of the room were cameras from four television stations, while one section of the seats was given up to the print and digital press. In front of the podium was a large group of immigrants and refugee rights activists. Near the door, in front of Caterina, was the mayor's staff and those elected city officials who supported Mayor Moretti on this issue.

"You've been busy," Caterina said to Taddeo Toddi. "It's a great turnout."

"It's raining and the river is getting high. Better to be here for a good cause," he said, then added, "There will be *crostini* and *vino* on the *Terrazzo di Saturno* after the speeches, of course."

Rafe came up behind Caterina in the doorway. "I thought I'd come for the final chapter of our little drama," he said over her shoulder as the mayor stood garnering polite, but restrained, applause.

Caterina made some room by taking a step forward, saying, "I hope this is just the beginning of something good for Mr. Nadja. He wanted to be in France, but maybe with a residency permit here, he will eventually get papers to travel more broadly."

Mayor Moretti started his speech by telling of the sad fate of a young American woman named Alice Perkins. Caterina heard Rafe curse quietly under his breath. She only caught part of the mayor's description of Adamou Nadja's bravery, as he put a hand on the shoulder of the man sitting in a chair beside the podium, because Rafe was pulling her backward out of the room.

"Rafe," she protested. "I want to hear this."

Rafe ignored her. "You didn't tell me the name of the woman in the Arno was Alice Perkins."

"What? Why is that important?" She thought back to the day that started with Rafe's call from the riverbank.

"I'm sure I told you about her over pizza at 'O Munaciello."

"You didn't say her name." They stopped at the top of a wide stone staircase, just out of the path of the flow of visitors touring the Palazzo Vecchio Museum. "Just that she was probably American. I don't think you knew her identity at that time."

"Right. In fact, we talked more about the party for Jake and Ross than we did about the drowning." Caterina stopped, staring off into the middle distance of memory and refocused on his face. "Again, why is that so important?"

"Remember the guy I thought I saw, but couldn't have seen."

"Because he's dead, right?"

"That's the one." Rafe's face was the picture of frustration. "His name was Adrian Rook."

Caterina nodded as if she was hearing the name for the first time. "What does Adrian Rook have to do with Alice Perkins?"

"Maybe nothing," admitted Rafe. "But if your drowned Alice Perkins was from Camden, Maine, then she's Rook's half sister."

"*Mio Dio*, Rafe!" She took his arm and urged him away from the stairway, through a door into an antechamber to the *Sala dei Duecento*. It was empty, but she could hear what must have been the end of the mayor's speech and the enthusiastic applause that followed it. She closed the door and turned, saying, "She had a Maine driver's license. Could it really be the same woman? That's one hell of a coincidence."

"What else do you know about her?" asked Rafe, looking like he wanted to shake the information out of her.

"Not much. She was twenty-four, had a passport issued recently, flew into Rome last Tuesday on an Alitalia flight from Boston." She paused, thinking hard. "Oh yeah, her father – a man named…"

"Lambert Perkins," Rafe said before she had a chance. "He lives somewhere in Vermont."

"Right. How do you know that? I just learned it at the American Consulate on Friday."

"I know everything there is to know about that bastard."

"Lambert Perkins?"

"No, Adrian Rook." The words poured out of him. "I know every school he ever went to, every man his mother married – there were three – as well as every job he held, all of the women he used and left behind, every country in which he did business in and most of the aliases he used. But Adrian Rook was his birth name and Alice Perkins was his mother's daughter by her third husband, Lambert Perkins. Reportedly, they were once close even though Alice was fifteen years younger than him. Their mother died of an opioid overdose last year."

"But you didn't know his sister was coming to Italy."

"He was dead!" Rafe exclaimed. "Why would I keep track of a sister he ignored after he left Camden, except to see her at their mother's funeral eighteen months ago."

"Let's get out of here." She led him down the stairway, through the Hall of the Five Hundred and down another stairway to the central courtyard of the palazzo.

"It's probably a coincidence, her being here. He's still dead. She was just on vacation, drank too much and fell into the Arno."

"I'm not buying it."

"Okay, let's get you all of the information we have on her," Caterina said. "I'm sure your friends at the Agency can dig up her itinerary and phone records. In fact, we should find out if the crime lab has been able to dry out her phone."

"Agency?" Rafe murmured. She almost missed it because he said it so quietly.

She stopped and turned on him before they walked out into the Piazza Signoria and the pouring rain. "Yes, the Agency. Let's quit dancing around this 'leave of absence, sabbatical' fairytale and deal with just the facts. Give me a bit of respect."

Rafe raised his hands as if to ward off her anger. "It's not something I can talk about and it's not something we can discuss together, either."

"So no 'discussion.'" She made air quotes with her fingers. "How about some yes or no answers?"

"Shoot."

"I'm right about your job?"

"Yes."

"Are you on a leave of absence now?"

"Sort of."

"Are you still in contact with your colleagues?"

"Yes."

"Did you tell them who you thought you saw Monday evening?"

"Yes."

"Do you think Adrian Rook is alive?"

"I don't know."

"Okay, let's go see Lt. Capra."

"Leo?"

"I forgot." She laughed out loud. "You already know Leo Capra from that case with Melissa Kincaid."

"I ate my first pizza in Florence with Leo and you."

They stepped out of the Palazzo Vecchio into the downpour. Caterina pulled a small umbrella out of the pocket of her raincoat.

"It's going to be faster to walk than get a cab," she said.

"It's just water." He put up the collar of his jacket and set off across the piazza.

"Once we get to the other side in the streets, hug the the walls," she advised. "Most of the buildings have an overhang at the roof line. It gives some protection."

When they crossed the Ponte Vecchio, the ancient configuration of the jewelry stores with shutters that closed like jewelry boxes gave some shelter although the crowds huddled near the display windows made for slow going. At the center of the bridge, where there was a large space between the shops, Rafe stepped under the cover of the Vasari Corridor, which had been constructed in 1565 over the original shops and ran the length of the bridge, and looked out at the roiling muddy water of the Arno.

"That is one angry river," he observed. "Any chance this is going to flood over its banks?"

Dead branches and other debris were becoming trapped at the abutments at each end of the bridge. Water washed over the boat ramp of the rowing club located upriver under the Uffizi Gallery. The tall steel doors were closed on the storage area where sculls, dragon boats and *barchetti* were stored. The lawn of the club was being threatened by the waves.

She nodded and urged him on to the Oltrarno. "There's always a chance. Someday I'll have my father tell you the story of 1966."

CHAPTER TWENTY-TWO

Leo Capra was able to give Rafe a clean towel from his gym bag, but was not able to provide much more information about Alice Perkins.

"With Caterina's help we contacted her father, but he hasn't gotten back to the U.S. Consulate with any decision about what to do with her body. Unfortunately, he has no legal responsibility for her burial or repatriation of her remains. We will keep her in the morgue for thirty days and then have her buried in a communal plot if he declines to give us any further directions." He carried the evidence box with her name and the case number written across one end into a small conference room. After signing the chain of custody document taped to the lid, he opened it. "Here's what we have: her purse, wallet with one credit card and driver's license, clothes – they are pretty disgusting, still damp and dirty – one shoe, passport, a brush and a cosmetic bag, and her airplane ticket. The crime lab still has her cell phone."

"Didn't she have a suitcase?" said Caterina, staring down at the meager contents of the box. "Surely she didn't come to Italy with just a big purse."

"We assume she did, but we don't know where she was staying. Her passport wasn't logged in by any hotel. Probably she was using an Airbnb or VRBO rental. Since it was deemed to be an accidental death, not a lot of effort has gone into finding her possessions. They will probably turn up in the next couple of weeks. They usually do in these cases. Somebody reports a missing renter at check out time."

"It seems like she is falling through the bureaucratic cracks here," observed Rafe.

Lt. Capra nodded. "She has in a way." He looked at Caterina. "Her case is assigned to Captain Ventroni in the San Frediano precinct, but we got most of her effects because of the potential theft of her bag."

"Theft?" Rafe enquired.

"We detained an Australian – Donald Mundt – for trespass on the Ponte Santa Trinita. When the officers brought him in, he had Alice Perkins' bag and its contents. The rest of her effects, basically what she was wearing, were sent over later because Ventroni didn't want to store them once he closed his file on the matter. You are absolutely right about that man, Caterina. A lazy racist. I may not have a stellar boss like your magistrate, but if I had to work for Ventroni, I would be putting in for a transfer to Pisa or Siena."

"What happened to Mundt?" asked Rafe.

"Both Caterina and I interviewed him. It was determined by the appropriate magistrate that we had nothing to hold him on in regard to the death of Miss Perkins, so he was released after paying the fine for trespassing on the bridge. I think he said he planned to continue his travels on Sunday or Monday."

"Could I get a copy of his passport?" asked Rafe.

Leo Capra gave Caterina an inquiring glance. She nodded and said, "Rafe is working with the Consulate on something. He may be able to resolve your issue of what to do with Alice's remains." It was only a slight misstatement of the facts, she thought.

"I can give you his mug shot and fingerprints, too. We got them when we thought we might have a case for theft or worse." Leo left to get the copies and returned with a neat folder.

Rafe opened it to stare at the mug shot for a long couple of minutes. "I don't know him."

"Wouldn't expect you to, being that he's from Australia. From the stamps in his passport he has never been to the U.S.," said Lt. Capra.

"Rafe knows a lot of people," Caterina said, nonsensically. "If you don't mind, Leo, I'm going to sign out Alice's wallet and passport, as well as ask the lab to send me her phone."

"Not a problem for me," he said. "If you can resolve the last issues of her case, I'd be grateful. Maybe you could have another go at her father."

She stood, signed the chain of custody sheet, slipped the items into an evidence bag, and placed it in her briefcase. "I'm going to take Rafe to the osteria for lunch to warm him up after his soaking. Do you want to join us?"

"Another time, thanks. We're on something called 'flood watch' that mandates we cancel all leave and maintain hyper vigilance in and around the Arno. If much more debris comes down the river, we may have to close one or more of the bridges just as a safety precaution. Why anyone thought it was a good idea to let trees and bushes grow along the walls next to the Arno, I can't say. Also, there are a couple of potential sink holes forming on the *lungarno*."

Caterina laughed. "You better hope the dam holds."

Rafe stopped and turned in the doorway to the small conference room, looking from one to the other of the two Florentine police officers.

"What dam?"

CHAPTER TWENTY-THREE

Cosimo Falcone leaned back in his chair, warming to his topic, "We just call it '*L'Alluvione*' because most everyone here, who is old enough, remembers that morning just over fifty years ago when the Arno River spilled over its banks. There is only one flood that is known as *the flood*. I was in my first year at university here in the city, living at home, of course. We had a front row seat to the devastation.

"Water and sludge, fuel oil and debris, animal carcasses and even cars were carried along by the floodwaters pouring over the river walls into the historic center. The water blew through the shops on the Ponte Vecchio, but those were the only store owners that got any warning that the wave was coming, so they got their gold and jewelry out. It came at night like a big wave because the floodgates to the dam upstream stuck open, emptying a lake of water. They say over 6,000 businesses were ruined because all of the shops are on the ground floor throughout the city. The water was over twenty feet deep, swirling around the Duomo and Santa Croce."

"You can still see the watermarks on the walls in certain places," Caterina added. "On the wall of the building at the corner of Piazza Santa Croce and Via Verdi are two plaques – the lower one for the 1557 flood and the higher one measuring the depth of the water in 1966 – that show how bad it really was."

"The Arno has flooded in a catastrophic manner eight times since 1333 – at a rate of about one a century, the one before 1966 was in 1844," said Cosimo. "My grandson told me that just last week. All of the school kids learn about the history of the river they cross every day."

"In 1966, it had been raining for days, just like this week." Caterina poured sparkling water from a carafe into three glasses. "Minor floods occur frequently – thirteen times since I was born – and still they do nothing about the shallowness of the riverbed."

"We just watched helplessly as the water rose," her father continued, ignoring her comment on the failure of governmental action "Since this was long before Facebook and Twitter, the response was slow. We were cut off from the government in Rome. A handful of amateur radio operators restored communications to help the authorities coordinate rescue efforts."

"My mother was doing a semester abroad in Florence. In the days after the flood she was a mud angel."

Rafe looked from father to daughter. "A mud angel? That doesn't sound like Margaret Mary Gifford Falcone." He reached for a piece of bread from the basket in the center of the table.

"That's what they called the foreigners and students who arrived to help dig out the city," explained Caterina.

Cosimo laughed, "She became my angel, too. You wouldn't have recognized her in her high rubber boots and a mud-smeared coat. I met her in line while we were salvaging books, parchments and scrolls from the basement of the National Library, passing them from hand to hand down the halls and up the stairs. The library was located where it is now, right next to the Arno. For centuries the most valuable documents were stored in the cool dry darkness of the lower levels. Worse luck for Florence, but the luckiest day of my life."

Lorenzo came out of the kitchen carrying a platter of *bruschetta* and chicken liver *crostini*. He placed it in the center of the table. "The problem in 1966, as I heard it," he said, "was that they just shoveled the mud back into the riverbed after the floodwaters receded. So now the Arno is just as shallow as it was then. The spillway to the dam may work these days, but there's still no place for excessive rainfall to go."

"That's comforting," said Rafe, before he took a bite of the toasted bread topped with chopped tomatoes, basil and olive oil. "I guess I should be looking for an apartment on a higher floor."

"Don't worry," said Caterina. "This side of the river and especially over at Piazza Tasso, where you live, is higher than the city center, so the water is unlikely to reach you." She winked at him. "Or, at least that's what our grandmother told us, claiming that it was so lucky that she and our grandfather decided to settle in the Oltrarno." She turned to her brother, requesting big bowls of *ribollita*, a hearty soup for a cold wet day. "Then maybe some warm *zabaione* for a sweet."

"I've got some roasted chicken with rosemary, if that sounds good to you."

"Not for me. I've got to get back to work. But maybe for Rafe." She raised an eyebrow at her still damp friend.

He nodded. "I'd appreciate it. The chicken would hit the spot. I just have to make a few calls from my place. They're waking up in D.C. right about now."

Lorenzo went back into the kitchen as Caterina explained to her father that Rafe was giving her some help in identifying the woman who drowned in the river. Cosimo popped another *crostini* in his mouth, wiped his hands on a napkin and went off to pick up a credit card from a customer who seemed seemed anxious to leave despite the rain pouring down outside the front window of Osteria da Guido.

CHAPTER TWENTY-FOUR

Patricia Benvenuti called out to Caterina as she stepped off the elevator at the Questura. "If you have a minute, my dear, would you sit and talk with me? I'm in a bit of a bind and thought you might have some advice."

Caterina crossed the reception area with its maroon Peshawar area rug and modern artwork, courtesy of the magistrate's collection. She dropped into the chair beside the administrative assistant's desk. The door to the magistrate's office was closed.

"What can I help you with, Pat?" she asked as she unbuttoned her raincoat and took off the fine woolen scarf from around her neck.

"I'm the chairwoman for the Florentine Craft Fair that the foreign consulates sponsor each year in November. This time it's at the U.S. consulate on Lungarno Amerigo Vespucci."

"I hope it's going to be held inside given that the rain doesn't seem to be ending anytime soon."

"Usually we use the courtyard, but the consulate has two big reception rooms that will work as well." Patricia stuck her pencil in the bun at the back of her head as was her habit. She opened a folder with lists of artisans who would be exhibiting at the fair. "The planning is mostly done."

"So why are you in a bind?"

"The Deputy Consul General who was arranging for the physical setup is pregnant. We thought we had enough time since she is due in December, but her doctor has some concerns and has put her on bed rest with strict instructions not to engage even in stressful thought, much less any activity." Patricia reached for her reading glasses that were on a gold chain around her neck and placed them on her nose. She peered through them at Caterina. "Susan Whitmore is short-staffed as it is. Her budget was cut this year for even the basic consular duties."

"How can I help?"

"I was hoping that the event planner that put together the party at Museo Stibbert might be free to step in at the last minute."

"She's certainly capable and has experience with large venues," said Caterina. "You might know her parents — the Forzonis."

"I know her father a bit. Real estate, right? His wife hasn't been seen recently or, at least, as far as I know."

"There was a death in the family a year or so ago. A son. Maybe that's why Beatrice's mother hasn't been out so much." Caterina picked up her purse and found her wallet inside. "I think I have her card." After searching for a minute, she handed a business card to Patricia.

Reaching for her glasses, only to find them already in place, she said, "Perfect. Do you think she will take on our project?"

"If she doesn't have a conflict, I would guess that she would. Feel free to tell her that I referred you."

Patricia clipped the card to the folder. "Do you think you could join us for the final planning meeting at my house this Saturday? I'm serving lunch."

"Even if you weren't serving one of your famous repasts, I'd love to join you."

Patricia slipped the folder away and as Caterina got up to leave, she said, "The magistrate asked that you join him and Marco at three this afternoon. I gather that Marco has a report from the anti-terrorist task group that may have some bearing on your Stibbert case."

"It's not really my case, but I'll certainly be here for the meeting."

When she slipped into the magistrate's office a couple minutes after three, Marco Capponi was already giving his report.

"... ISIS-affiliated Facebook page with threats against the Vatican, but we deem this to be little more than an effort to incite home grown terror activity, rather than an active threat in the planning stages." Marco flipped over a page in his notebook and tapped it with his silver pen. "Of course," he said, not pausing as Caterina slipped into the other chair, "we are urging all law enforcement agencies to be on the lookout for threats against soft targets such as the Uffizi, the Accademia, or any of the major churches."

"Has there ever been any Islamic terror threat in Florence," asked Caterina.

"Not specifically, but with the flood of illegal immigrants from Islamic states, it is only a matter of time," Marco asserted.

The magistrate frowned as he listened, then asked, "Does the anti-terrorist task force actually think that this influx of refugees is breeding a hotbed of terrorists? That radicalized individuals with the aim of terrorizing Florence or Rome are risking their own lives in overloaded boats launched by human smugglers?"

Marco's shoulders hunched in defense, as he blustered, "There is some evidence that the miscreants that targeted the airport in Belgium came through Lampedusa or one of the Greek islands. They hid among the women and children and passed on through to the ultimate target."

"Some evidence or strong evidence?"

Marco didn't answer.

"I heard something the other day," Caterina said without sourcing the information, "about the Calabrian 'Ndràngheta outfitting ISIS in Syria and Libya with arms. Did that come up in any of your meetings, Marco?"

"In fact, it did," he answered, staring at her before looking for the precise page in his notebook. "There was an interesting connection with a Florentine family. It's a name you will know, Caterina – Mollica."

The name did seem familiar, but it didn't immediately come to Caterina's mind where she had heard it before. "Mollica?"

"Leone Mollica. Lives in San Frediano not far from your place, I believe."

"Be a little more clear, Marco, " said his boss. "What is the interest of the task force?"

Caterina leaned forward. "I remember. Leone Mollica is the uncle of Timo Monti, the young man who was killed at the Stibbert Museum."

"It seems I may be working that case with you," Marco said. "I have requested access to the files."

"I'm hardly working the case." Caterina sat back. "My role is only as an observer. It's Captain Gentile's case out in the Montughi precinct. He's working a theory that it was a falling out between thieves. Stolen goods were found in the victim's car."

"I may be able to elucidate a more logical hypothesis." Marco was assuming his usual pompous persona, Caterina thought. "Once I provide Gentile with the task force's resources, I'm sure he will see the wisdom of the inquiry."

"Has the anti-terrorism task force asked you to interject yourself into the Stibbert investigation," asked Paolo Benigni. "I thought you were just auditing their meetings to keep us better informed to do our work here."

"But, sir," sputtered Marco. "We are involved in the Stibbert case. Caterina was on the scene at the time of the murder. My work with the task force can only be of the most necessary assistance."

"Okay, Marco. Lay it out for us. How do the activities of Leone Mollica result in the death of his nephew?"

"I haven't worked it all out, yet, but we do know that Mollica, who is originally from Naples, owns a number of stands in the San Lorenzo market that he leases out to various vendors, some of whom are Italian and others of Middle Eastern descent. Mollica regularly takes possession of shipments of leather goods and other items at the port in Naples. Those shipments come from Morocco and Egypt. Recent investigations have focused on the contents of the shipments he sends in the other direction. His nephew has been working as a truck driver for the business ever since he left high school two years ago."

Caterina thought of Rafe's claim that he had seen the arms dealer Adrian Rook in the garden of the Villa Stibbert. Could he have been there meeting Timo Monti the night of the party? Did Rook know the Seal Team who had targeted him in Homs and Rafe, who suffered at his hands, were there? Or was it just some weird cosmic coincidence? More likely Rook, if he were alive, wasn't in Italy at all. But what was his half-sister doing in Florence? She was going to discuss these issues with Rafe before she ever brought them up with Marco.

While Caterina was pondering her own questions, the magistrate was warning Marco not to tread on the investigational toes of Captain Gentile, reminding him that it was counterproductive to take a slim set of unproven facts and try to prove a theory that so far lacked any support. He did, however, allow Marco to review the Stibbert homicide files he had already requested.

"Marco, I insist that you keep Caterina informed of any progress or even any thoughts you have on this matter, before you share them with Captain Gentile's team."

CHAPTER TWENTY-FIVE

Caterina, heeding the magistrate's cautionary words, decided to contact Max, not Rafe, about the suspicion that Leone Mollica and his nephew were engaged in smuggling arms from Italy to North Africa.

"I assume Rafe is actually working during his 'sabbatical' and you will share with him any pertinent information regarding Mollica's operation and this mysterious Adrian Rook," she added, after she laid out Marco's findings and suspicions. "You've dealt with Marco before, so you know how reliable, or not, he can be."

"Or not," echoed Max. "Of course, there's always the danger of underestimating Marco. His goal of becoming the youngest *commissario* in the Florence police force has led to good investigative results in the past. He tends to make intuitive leaps that are either precisely right or grossly wrong. I'll check this through our channels and see what comes up."

"Are you keeping in touch with Captain Gentile?"

"Of course," Max said with a wry chuckle. "I *always* follow up on murders that take place at parties I attend. So far it seems that the death had little or nothing to do with the party guests, which makes it easier. However, with Rafe's sighting of the ghost of Adrian Rook, I don't want to make any assumptions. I'm tracking police and intelligence reports from Florence."

"It's important for me to keep my boss in the loop, so please let me know if there's anything I should be reporting to him. No surprises."

"I totally understand and won't leave you hanging," Max assured her. He paused and then added, "Don't overthink the Rafe situation."

"What Rafe situation?"

"His job. What did you think I meant?"

"Exactly that," Caterina responded, glad that he couldn't see her blush. "I just wish he would be more candid with me."

"The Agency constantly warns all employees that once they share information with anyone, friend or foe, they lose control of that information. Even if it is simply who they work for. Rafe has more reason than most to be reticent. It's not that he doesn't trust you."

"I hope not. I'm trusting him with another investigation I have."

"The woman in the river."

Caterina voiced her surprise, "How do you know that, Max?"

"See what I mean about losing control of information," Max said. "Rafe called me right after lunch, looking for information about Donald Mundt and Alice Perkins."

"I can't imagine you would know much about Mr. Mundt. He's Australian."

"And Alice Perkins is American, so I should have gotten a memo from you as soon as you learned that fact, right?"

"You are so right. I'm sorry. I guess I just thought, since it was an accidental death…"

"Don't worry, Caterina. I'm just yanking your chain, so to speak." He laughed. "As for Mundt being Australian, Rafe, in an abundance of caution, is checking out that very fact. He wants all of the agencies to run facial recognition on your bridge trespasser."

Caterina was left to ponder the meaning of this because at that moment Patricia Benvenuti transferred a call from Detective Castagna about the break-in of the French girls' apartment on Via Taddea.

"The high-top shoes were the key and the rental agency was the lock that needed to be opened," he said with a self-satisfied tone.

No one ever said criminals were smart, Caterina thought as she listened to the story unfold. The receptionist at the rental agency was wearing Celine Plantier's opal pendant on its gold chain as she blithely went about her duties, not knowing it was stolen. She was happy to tell the friendly young police officer that her boyfriend, the agency's handyman, had given it to her for the three month anniversary of their first date. The handyman, Pino Buttari, was wearing purple and white striped high-tops, as a loyal follower of the city's soccer club, when he answered her call to stop by the office at the officer's behest.

The laptop and the Samsung tablet were long gone, but the burglary squad was able to nab Pino's confederate and the fence they were using to dispose of the stolen items. Massimo Castagna had personally returned Celine's necklace and secured a date for the next Saturday evening.

The owner of the agency had no involvement in the scheme. She merely thought the rash of burglaries at the apartments she managed was a symptom of the fact that theft was the most common crime in Italy. She showed the detectives the documents that she gave to every client that said in bold letters that tenants should never let strangers into the common areas of the apartment buildings and never into the apartments, themselves. The warnings went on to include instructions about the multiple bolt locks on the doors and how to secure the windows.

After congratulating Det. Castagna on the speedy resolution of the case, Caterina asked Patricia to resend the task force's annual directive to the many foreign schools in Florence warning of apartment burglaries, pick-pockets, and bicycle thefts, as well as a general, but largely unheeded, admonition about the personal safety hazards of walking the streets of the city late at night while alone or intoxicated.

Depressed by the seventh day of rain, not ready to face the damp commute across the city in an overcrowded bus, Caterina pulled out the *Corriere della Sera* she had snagged at the osteria from her father. The forecast was brighter for the upcoming weekend, but the effect of constant downpour was dire. A sinkhole had opened along Lungarno Torrigiani, east of the Ponte Vecchio, swallowing a Fiat 500 and two Vespas. There was some thought that the apartments in the palazzos bordering that stretch of the Arno would have to be evacuated. They were cut off from water and sewage service for the time being. The underground telephone and electrical lines were being evaluated as the rocks and soil protecting them sloughed away into the river.

"When the *acqua alta* comes, I'm always glad that I live in Settignano, high above the city," said Patricia when Caterina, on her way out of the office, showed her the article.

"But it's so dramatic to look down from my parents' terrace and watch the space under the arches of the Ponte Vecchio get smaller and smaller," Caterina teased.

"My husband described how his antique shop on Via Maggio just escaped the 1966 flood by ten meters. The mud closed the street and there he was – safe – but for how long? Of course, at the time they didn't know about the dam. They thought the river would just keep rising."

"Some of his competitors must have lost their inventory."

"Not many. He and others opened their storerooms for the ones closer to the river. They passed all of the treasures down the street from hand to hand. The

Oltrarno flooded much less than the city center. Even I, in Australia, saw the photographs of the panels torn off Ghiberti's Doors on the Baptistry."

Caterina settled in the chair beside Patricia's desk. "When did you get to Florence?"

"About fifteen years after the flood. I was doing graduate work in art history," Patricia said as she started clearing off her desk for the evening. "Pietro was much older than me. He took me under his wing, offering me a job in his shop. I had an apartment in the palazzo across the street. Love came later, sooner for him than for me, but I do admit he was a charmer from day one."

"I bet he was," Caterina said as she rose, picking up her briefcase, purse, raincoat and umbrella from the floor beside her chair. "I'm off."

"I forgot." Patricia held a file folder. "I compiled this for you." She handed it to Caterina. "Marco asked me to do what he called 'a deep dive' into the last five years of information about Leone Mollica and Timo Monti. Although how I am supposed to dive into a computer, I can't tell you." She watched Caterina thumb through the printouts. "I made a copy for you, since it is technically your case. The magistrate asked me to keep an eye on Marco's progress. I thought you could help me with that."

"You're a gem, Patricia." Caterina slipped the file into her briefcase. "I'll look at this tonight. Although I'm pretty comfortable with Captain Gentile's approach, who knows which way some random info will lead Marco."

CHAPTER TWENTY-SIX

Caterina, dressed in an extra-large red Boston University sweatshirt over black stretch leggings topped with bulky red knitted socks, chopped celery, onion, and carrots so fine that even her father couldn't complain. Or so she told herself as she poured the extra virgin olive oil into a pan to heat before adding the vegetables with a dash of salt and cracked pepper. As her *soffritto* transformed into a soft translucent fragrant sauce, she cut up five small porcini mushrooms and an equal amount of cremini mushrooms. She added them to the pot with some fresh thyme and garlic and stirred as it cooked down a bit, before pouring in a couple of cups of chicken stock.

While the soup bubbled she opened a good bottle of an Aglianico varietal from Basilicata. Turning back to the stove she added a few more porcini slices to the soup because she liked the variation in texture of well-cooked and under-cooked ingredients. Then she poured a quarter cup of cream into the pot and added a big pat of butter because an autumn soup should be thick and rich. When she was too hungry to wait, she ladled the mushroom soup into a ceramic bowl.

The crowning moment came, she thought, as she dotted the top with truffle oil and used a truffle shaver to add a mound of paper-thin slices of the tiny white truffle that she had taken from the osteria four days before. A couple of pieces of golden, oily, salty focaccia from the bakery down the block, just right for catching the last dregs of soup, finished the meal.

Later, in bed with the contents of Patricia's file spread around her and a last glass of the deep red wine in one hand, Caterina, only a bit sleepy, started to learn about Leone Mollica and Timo Monti. She read the report from Captain Gentile again. Mollica was from Naples and his wife was born in Calabria. They had lived in Florence's San Frediano district, about five blocks from Caterina's address, for over ten years and had a fifteen-year-old daughter. For the last four years, Mollica's nephew Timo had been living with the family in Florence.

From Patricia's research, Caterina learned that for all of the time Mollica had been in Florence his business had been registered as an import/export venture, but in the most recent years he acquired a number of stalls in the San Lorenzo market. Caterina knew that these licenses issued by the city required an outlay of a considerable sum. She wondered where had he gotten the funds.

Leone owned two panel trucks. Marco had requested a year's worth of Telepass data for the Mollica trucks traveling on the Autostrada from Florence to Naples. He also wanted a map with locations of all of the Italian military armory warehouses. Caterina assumed he was going to try to correlate the itineraries with the warehouses. She decided to leave that work to him.

Captain Gentile's report revealed that Timo Monti lived with his uncle's family while he attended high school at *Istituto Scolastico Sacra Famiglia* and then remained after graduation. Patricia had acquired Timo's school records and talked to the registrar. Her typed notes revealed that Timo was an average student who had trouble making friends in the first year, but did better after that. The registrar told Patricia that Timo Monti almost didn't graduate because he had been in a traffic incident involving a race in the *viale* near the Fortezza da Basso during final exams. He eventually received his diploma, but decided not to go on to university.

Caterina jotted a note to herself to get the full report of the traffic infraction. After graduation, Timo got a commercial driver's certificate that allowed him to drive the Mollica company's trucks. Marco had requested a schedule for Timo Monti's routes to Naples and back for the last year. Patricia hadn't yet separated out Timo's trips from those of other drivers.

Patricia had googled Timo Monti and found an announcement from a mixed martial arts school that revealed Timo had completed the basic certification course. The website for the *Calcio Storico Fiorentino* listed Timo Monti as a member of the Santo Spirito *Bianchi* squad. Caterina now understood how Timo's nose had been broken, perhaps more than once, and why he had recent tattoos. A web page of photographs of *Calcio Storico Fiorentino tatuaggi* showed off the impressive ink sported by the four teams of the historical soccer game. The teams of sportsmen were also known to be violent petty criminals.

With these thoughts Caterina began to have questions about Captain Gentile's theory of the case that Timo Monti was a thief, who was killed in the commission of a crime. Timo had a history of theft. The fact that his juvenile crimes were handled privately explained why his fingerprints weren't in the crime database, but as Caterina looked over the list of prints found at the Stibbert Museum and on the evidence in Leone Mollica's car, it didn't add up. Timo's prints were on the suit of armor he was wearing and on the car's steering wheel, but not on the hatchback of the car or the the stolen items or the shopping bag used to carry the purloined goods. Captain Gentile's report explained the lack of Timo's prints employing the theory that he used gloves while stealing the items. But no gloves were found at the murder scene, in the car, or in the cantina. There were two unidentifiable prints found on the Gucci shopping bag, one near the handle and another on the base.

It also bothered Caterina that the report concluded that Timo Monti stole from the Stibbert Museum. How did he even know about the collection? She was the first to admit that most Florentine children were familiar with the museum because it was a favorite spot from an early age. But Timo grew up in Perugia and it was unlikely that the friars at *Istituto Scolastico Sacra Famiglia* took senior level students to that museum. The Mollica household lived in the San Frediano neighborhood, far from the museum. Of course, Caterina thought, Timo may have had an accomplice who was both familiar with the museum and knew how to steal from the collection without being detected. But who was the accomplice? One of the helpers Beatrice Forzoni hired? Maybe, she thought, Marco's theory of an organized crime connection was more plausible.

This led Caterina to think about the items that were stolen. Why those items? The collection at the Stibbert Museum gave every appearance that precious objects could be picked up at will, but in reality all of the small articles and *objet d'art* were locked in display cabinets, and the other exhibition items were too heavy to carry away with any ease. Also, when the museum was open, visitors had to go through with a guide. During the party there were helpers in every major room and others wandering at random. Any theft would have happened after the scavenger hunt was over and the party guests were sitting down to dinner.

Caterina thumbed through the pages of Captain Gentile's report, but there was no description of where in the museum the stolen items had been taken. She knew they weren't from the Hall of the Cavalcade where Timo was found. She wondered why the victim went back into the museum after he had gotten the valuables out? To get more treasures? Why were those particular items taken? Was the purpose of the costume to hide in plain sight, and how did a truck driver know about the costume? There were too many questions and she had drunk too much wine to make any more sense of it all. She gathered the various reports together and set them aside.

The last thought Caterina had before she went to sleep was that she hoped Patricia had been able to retain Beatrice Forzoni for the Florentine Craft Fair and that Bea would be at the planning lunch on Saturday. Surely she could answer some of these questions about Timo and the theft.

CHAPTER TWENTY-SEVEN

The Arno claimed two lives the next day, Thursday. One from a car accident in the eastern suburb of the city where a small road along the river flooded. A teenager, going home in the early morning hours from his family's pizzeria, skidded off the embankment into the river.

The second death appeared, during the initial investigation, to be a drowning. The body of a man, thought to be in his mid-thirties, was found caught in the submerged rose bushes on the lawn of the rowing club.

The *Società Canottieri Firenze*, located under the Uffizi, had been closed for five days because the Arno's current had become too dangerous for the two-man sculls, kayaks or the pole-guided *barchetto* to be out on the river. Day by

day the muddy water had crept up over the dock and the
lawn where dinner was served in the summer, to the
bushes near the wall, and finally, to the high brick
retaining wall with its chipping plaster.

The body was discovered by the private security
guard who patrolled the Ponte Vecchio from midnight to
dawn, protecting the jewelry shops from break-ins and
vandalism. The coroner said the man had probably been
in the river for three or four hours, but that he had not
drowned. There was no water in his lungs and a small
wound on the back of his neck was quite deep, probably
caused by a long narrow knife being shoved up into his
brain. The coroner wrote that he was impressed at the
skill or luck it took to avoid hitting the skull or cervical
vertebrae with the insertion of the blade.

Caterina read the coroner's report online in the
secure police reporting files after Marco brought it to her
attention. Marco was interested because he had recently
followed a case where a Syrian had been found in bed at
the posh Four Seasons Hotel with a stiletto in the back of
his neck. The man in the Arno was not a case that was
going to be assigned to their task force because the
documents in the victim's wallet included an Italian
driver's license and a *carta d'identità*, for a forty-year-old
named Antonio Bevilaqua, as well as credit cards in the
same name. The rest of the contents of his wallet had
been scanned into the file, which was where one item
caught Caterina's attention. Among the money, receipts,
and business cards, was a photo of a very young, blonde
Alice Perkins.

The magistrate was not in the office. Patricia said he was going to be out until five at a conference of the *Associazione Generale fra i Magistrati d'Italia* being held at the new judicial courthouse, the *Tribunale Ordinario,* near the airport. Caterina decided to call Max Turner for advice.

"I'll catch a train within the hour," he said after she had laid out the facts as she knew them and described the odd coincidence of the murder of the Syrian gentleman. "Can you get that file from Marco? And call Rafe. Don't tell him what it's about, but have him come to the Questura by four. Even if this is just a look-alike Alice Perkins in the photo, I want Rafe to get a look at the body from the river. This may be her half-brother using an Italian alias."

"You can't think Rafe has anything to do with either death, do you?"

"No, but if there is even the slightest chance that your body is Adrian Rook there are certainly going to be questions. I want to get ahead of this. I've got to go if I want to catch the next train. See you in a couple of hours."

She called Rafe and he didn't even ask why she wanted to see him, but said instead, "I was just going to call you. There's something interesting about that Mundt guy, the Australian, you know."

"What?"

"It would be better if I come to your office and lay it out for you. Also, your boss should probably see the information I got from Langley and Interpol," he said. "I'll be there by four."

By this point, Caterina was too nervous to leave her boss out of the loop. She sent him a text, asking him to call, which he did twenty minute later.

"I have about five minutes, Caterina. What is the problem?"

"It may be nothing, sir." She gave him just the facts, but added a bit about Rafe's experience in Homs with Adrian Rook. She told him that she had contacted the Americans.

Throughout her recitation the magistrate said nothing. When she finished, he was quiet for a minute and then said, "I can't say that I am not disappointed that the situation has gotten to this point before you thought to discuss it with me. You lack experience in your position, so I expect to be kept informed before you involve individuals outside the task force."

"I understand, sir," she said, her stomach knotting. "But I thought…"

He interrupted, "That being said, I believe that the most efficient way to resolve this tangled mass of seemingly unrelated events, but with odd similarities, is to get everyone who has a piece of the puzzle in a room together."

"Uh, yes, yes, sir," she stammered. "By everyone, you mean…?"

"If this new body turns out to be a friend of Alice Perkins, or is related to her, then the Americans can help. If the common method of the killings is pertinent, Marco should be included, as should the homicide detective handling the Four Seasons' case and the officer investigating the rowing club homicide."

"I think that's going to be Leo Capra, since he wrote up the original report this morning," she interjected. "I'll ask Marco to call his contact on the Syrian's homicide."

"Can you think of anyone else we should include?"

Caterina hoped she wasn't missing someone obvious when she said, "No, sir."

"Neither can I, but before you get all of these people around a table, what should be your next line of inquiry?"

Caterina's mind went blank. She stumbled through the possibilities, saying, "Well, sir, I guess since we may be dealing with a known arms-dealer, that the anti-terrorism…"

"Think more concretely, Caterina. Don't make this theoretical. Marco will take care of that." Caterina could swear she heard a smile in his voice. "What are the facts?" he insisted.

"Two men killed in a similar manner."

"Yes, and what about the other body?"

"At the Stibbert Museum?"

"No, the other body in the river."

"Alice Perkins?"

"You have a photograph of one person found in the river in the wallet of another person found in the river. What should your question be?"

"I should be asking if her death is related to his, if it was really a murder, not an accident."

"Exactly."

"But the coroner deemed it an accidental drowning."

"In my experience, coroners tend to look for what they expect to find. In the first case there was an intoxicated American woman who had river water in her lungs."

"You think they didn't look for any wounds."

"Did she have long hair?

"Yes."

"So…?" He waited.

"I should ask the coroner to check the back of her neck."

CHAPTER TWENTY-EIGHT

Paolo Benigni assured Caterina that he would be back at the Questura in time to take part in the late afternoon meeting of all of the interested players in the Arno cases. "This conference is damn boring," he had said.

She called the coroner's office and made a request for a quick reexamination of the body of Alice Perkins, especially the occipital area of her head. Dr. DiPiero, sounding both irritated and intrigued, agreed to do it immediately, especially after Caterina suggested that he compare any findings with the hole at the base of the skull of Antonio Bevilaqua, who resided in one of his other refrigerated drawers. He also acquiesced when she asked for additional photographs of Mr. Bevilaqua's face and the tattoo on the outside of his upper left arm that was described in the original report.

Next she called the crime lab and asked the technician who was skilled with phones and computers if she had been able to dry out and access Alice Perkins' phone. Receiving an affirmative response, Caterina inquired about the possibility of getting print-outs of the text messages and calls. The technician told her that the cell phone was basically new so the data was minimal. She said she would send an email with a couple of attachments within a few minutes.

Patricia Benvenuti looked in Marco's files and found the officer – Lt. Franco Banfi – responsible for the homicide investigation into the death of Syrian businessman Walid Asfari. She called him and Lt. Capra, invoking the magistrate's name, to request their presence at the Questura at half past four. That being done, Caterina finally went to see Marco Capponi.

Marco was a bit miffed that he was being informed of his expected participation at a meeting where the agenda was already set, but he soon recovered when he realized that his theory about a connection between Leone Mollica and arming of terrorists would get a fair airing. He hadn't connected his earlier case, involving Mr. Asfari's death, with the Museo Stibbert killing of Mollica's nephew, but within a minute he had it all figured out.

"I initially thought Asfari was just a multi-millionaire following his wife to Italy on a shopping excursion," he told Caterina, who was sitting across from his desk, thinking she had some time before the results came through from the crime lab and the coroner. "Asfari's wife told Lt. Banfi and me that she thought he had been killed by a hooker. I guess when they traveled, she shopped and he screwed around. It seemed like an arrangement that worked for her."

The top of Marco's desk was completely clear except for a leather desk set and a silver clock. In the corner behind the chair Caterina was sitting in, was a small side table on top of which was his outbox, stacked high with paper and files. In the close confines of his office, small like her own, his aftershave with notes of bergamot, jasmine and musk wafted around her, not unpleasant, just strong. He had once told her it was a cologne inspired by Emperor Napoleon, which she found very apropos given his height and attitude.

Caterina hadn't been paying much attention, but the suspected culprit in the Syrian's death, however, struck her as absurd. "You didn't actually believe that a prostitute would shove a knife into the base of a client's skull, did you?"

"Not really," Marco admitted. "But we were getting a lot of push back from the Quirinale in Rome."

"Why would the Italian government want to support that theory of the case?" Caterina was intrigued enough to give him another five minutes of her attention.

"You probably didn't notice, since you are a bit provincial," Marco said.

"Provincial?" Caterina snorted. Dammit, she thought, I went to university in the U.S. and have relatives working in academia and governments in three countries. She knew Marco's father was an office clerk and his uncle was a high-ranking officer in the Florence Questura, but

Marco had never traveled outside of Italy. Who was provincial?

"You know what I mean. Your family runs an osteria. You are only interested in food and your brother's children. You never talk about politics." He stopped, as if his case was made. "So you probably did not know that during the last Italian government, the one in power last year, high level members of the interior ministry undertook secret meetings with Bashar al-Assad's top military advisors."

Marco had surprised her. He was right, she didn't know of any such meetings that surely would have violated Italy's agreements with her EU counterparts. She said so, and then asked, "And that is related to your dead Syrian, how?"

"Asfari was on the plane Italy sent to bring Ali Mamlouk, the head of Syria's national security bureau, to Rome. Mamlouk is on an EU restricted entry list."

"So some time later, Asfari is killed and the new Italian government does not want the connection to be made," Caterina said. "No wonder his death didn't make the local papers."

"Or the national ones either," added Marco. "The investigation was wrapped up quickly and my job was just to get the body and the family back to Damascus." He thought about it for a moment, then smiled. "Which I did."

"But now we have one, maybe two, other foreigners with the same mode of death, within a week of Mr. Asfari's assassination."

"Not assassination. Unfortunate death."

"Why?"

"Because there can be no connection between Asfari and arms dealing with ISIS, even in Syria." He looked chagrined to see the magistrate's administrative assistant standing in his doorway.

"Don't worry, Marco. You know I never listen to anything said in this office," Patricia said, winking at Caterina as she handed over a few pages of printer paper. "I thought Caterina should see these. That nice girl, Alba, from the crime lab sent them over."

Caterina stood and started to follow Patricia out of the office, before turning to say to Marco, "You may want to get your story straight with Franco Banfi. I told you he's coming to the meeting this afternoon, didn't I?" She was gratified to see him reach immediately for the phone.

Caterina thumbed through the pages of cell phone texts and calls as she walked down the hall with Patricia, not quite listening, when the words "… Forzoni will be able to, I'm relieved to say" caught her attention.

"What was that, Patricia?"

"The Florentine Craft Fair. Beatrice Forzoni is going to run it for us. She'll be there on Saturday."

"Saturday?"

Patricia stopped, making sure she had Caterina's full attention. "Beatrice will be at my place for the final planning lunch with the committee. I know you are, as we say, 'underwater' with these Arno cases…" She patted the younger woman's shoulder and gave her a small smile. "So don't feel as if you have to be there."

"Sorry, Patricia. I wasn't paying attention. I'll be there 'come hell or high water,' as you also say." Caterina grinned. "These cases are not taking up that much of my time. Others are doing the real work. It's not like when I had to babysit that American woman, Melissa Kincaid, this past summer. I'll be there this Saturday," she repeated as she entered her office, only to step out again. "Patricia, could you do me a favor?"

"Yes?"

"Find me the report about the auto accident Beatrice's brother was in last year. My mother mentioned it and I didn't remember reading about it in the papers at the time. I don't want to bring it up with Beatrice, since it must be painful." She gave a shrug. "It's really none of my business, but I was curious. No rush. Just when you get a moment."

CHAPTER TWENTY-NINE

Alice Perkins had been texting with her half-brother, but what was more interesting to Caterina, as she read through the transcript provided by the technician, was the first text, dated only two weeks before the American's death, thanking Adrian for sending her a new cell phone and a ticket to Italy. Alice was excited about these "birthday presents" and looked forward to seeing him in Florence.

The next text was one Alice received from Adrian, asking her to bring a big suitcase so they could do some shopping. It also directed her to use the cell phone *only* for communicating with him. "Our private line" was how he put it.

Caterina noted the number Rook was calling from, but when she tried to ring it, the Italian cell phone number was out of service. She instructed Alba, the technician, to trace the phone, but wasn't optimistic. She assumed it was turned off or destroyed, but at least she could find out where Adrian Rook had been when he communicated with Alice.

There were two more chatty texts from Alice before she flew out from Boston. Her plan was to drive from Camden to the airport and park in the long-term lot. The second text was from the airport saying her plane was on time. To each text, Adrian responded "*K*."

Caterina's phone rang. It was Dr. DiPiero, the coroner.

"I do not know how I missed it," he said. "Of course, it was so damn small."

"What was, doctor?"

"The tiny hole in the hair line at the base of her skull that runs straight through her occipital orifice into her brain. This seemed to be such a simple case of a fatal fall that I did not see the need to shave her head during the first autopsy. I checked for needle marks and other obvious wounds, but there were only a few bruises from the fall."

"But you said she died from drowning. Wouldn't a knife wound to the brain kill her instantly, making it impossible to inhale water?"

"It depends on what you mean by 'instantly' because it would all depend on the timing and effect of the knife entering her cerebral cortex. If she was stabbed and thrown immediately into the Arno, her autonomic nervous control system could act on its own for up to a few minutes regulating bodily functions, such as the heart rate and respiratory rate. The wound did not bleed out, but into her skull."

Caterina was taking quick notes. She asked one last question, "Is the wound on Alice Perkins the same as on the body of the victim found at the rowing club?"

"Antonio Bevilaqua?"

"Yes."

"The depth and circumference and the angle of the wounds are the same. My assumption is that they were made by the same person, wielding the same weapon, but I would have to have the blade to examine to swear to this."

"Thank you, doctor," Caterina said. "I know you are going to send your report to Captain Ventroni, so he will reopen the case as a homicide. But would you also send a copy to Lt. Leo Capra at the Palazzo Pitti station and to Magistrate Benigni?" She paused. "I think your assistant is going to send me some photographs of Antonio Bevilaqua." Caterina looked up to see Patricia opening the door of her office for Rafe. She waved him to a chair as Dr. DiPiero said, "The photos should be in your email as we speak. The full report will be done this evening."

Rafe placed a file on her desk and as she hung up he said, "I have something you should…"

Caterina interrupted, saying, "Here look at these." She passed the copies of Alice Perkins' text messages. "Alice was texting with Adrian Rook just two weeks ago."

"Or someone she believed was Rook."

"I thought you were so sure he was alive." Caterina decided not to tell him about the second body in the Arno. Better to wait until the photographs arrived. She turned on her computer to check her email.

Rafe shook his head. "I'm not sure what I believe."

Caterina pointed to the last text in the series. "The odd thing is that if she was writing to Adrian, she was arranging to meet him last night."

"Last night? But she drowned a week ago." He took the sheet out of her hand. "You're right. The message was sent last Thursday in response to his text saying he would be in Florence 'next Wednesday' – that would have been yesterday. But that would mean that the last thing Alice did in a drunken stupor before she rolled off the Santa Trinita Bridge was to text her brother and stick her phone in her pocket. Impossible."

"Well, about that…" Caterina was going to tell him about Dr. DiPiero's findings when Max Turner walked into her office.

He put his hands on Rafe's shoulders, saying, "Sorry to interrupt. Caterina, let's move this to the conference room. I rode up in the elevator with the magistrate and he asked me to fetch you and find Rafe. Marco is already there polishing that fancy silver pen of his."

"What the hell are you doing here, Max?" Rafe looked from the face of his friend to Caterina and back.

"I may be on a fool's errand, but my gut tells me it's more serious than that. Come on."

CHAPTER THIRTY

Caterina made Paolo Benigni laugh when she walked into the conference room, took an exaggerated look at her watch and raised an inquiring eyebrow.

"The conference was boring," he explained. "I left before the last two sessions. One was about budgeting for new cases and the other was a discussion of the appropriate robes and tassels we have to wear at the opening of the Year of the Judiciary next month."

Lt. Leo Capra stood as she approached the table. With a smile, she passed a copy of Alice Perkins' text messages across to him. "You'll be especially interested in the timing of the last message."

Patricia Benvenuti came in behind Rafe and Max. She was escorting a short bald man in a lieutenant's uniform, who introduced himself as Franco Banfi. Patricia handed Caterina a file, saying that it was the photographs sent over by Oscar, the coroner's assistant.

Marco waved Lt. Banfi over to his side of the table. The magistrate took a seat at the end and Caterina sat down flanked by Rafe and Max. That left the other end to Leo Capra, but he decided to decline the honor and took a chair next to Banfi.

Magistrate Benigni started by saying that the *Task Force per gli stranieri* was taking the lead on the coordination of the three cases because it appeared that three foreigners – Alice Perkins, Walid Asfari, and Antonio Bevilaqua, aka Adrian Rook – had all been assassinated in Florence by the same killer or, at least, in the same manner.

"What?" said Rafe at the same time Lt. Capra said, "But what do you mean, Antonio Bevilaqua is someone called Adrian Rook?"

"What man in the river?" Rafe asked again.

"Let me clarify the situation as we know it, so that we are all working off the same set of facts," said the magistrate. "Tuesday, a week ago, Walid Asfari was murdered at the Four Seasons Hotel when a stiletto was shoved through the back of his neck up into his brain. The knife was left in place. The cause of death was clear."

"I know Walid Asfari," said Rafe. "He's tight with Assad. You say he was murdered? I didn't hear about it."

"Let me finish, Mr. Mathews," admonished Paolo Benigni. "On Thursday of that week, Alice Perkins, from the state of Maine in the U.S., was found in the Arno. Today, we discovered that she didn't drown by accident, but was murdered – a stab wound to the back of her neck. This morning, the body of a man, carrying the identification of one Antonio Bevilaqua, was found on the flooded ground of the rowing club near the Ponte Vecchio. He, too had a wound to the back of his neck. Unlike Ms. Perkins, he had no river water in his lungs, therefore the coroner has determined that he was dead before he was thrown into the Arno."

Rafe looked at Caterina, while waving the transcript of the texts, "Last night was the planned rendezvous of Alice Perkins and Adrian Rook."

"Who is Adrian Rook?" asked Marco.

"An arms dealer," answered Lt. Banfi. "He does business in Syria and Libya and has ties to the 'Ndràngheta clans."

Everybody at the table turned to look at Franco Banfi. Rafe and Max seemed to wonder why this small uniformed man knew so much about an American arms dealer. Caterina was curious about whether Lt. Banfi had taken Marco into his confidence about the dealings between the mafia and ISIS, but discarded that thought seeing the blank look on Marco's face. The magistrate seemed just to want a common understanding between all of the participants at the table.

"Is that intelligence from the Asfari file?" asked Marco. "Why didn't I…"

"It was on a need to know basis. You didn't need to know it to get Asfari's body and his family out of Italy and back to Damascus." Banfi made eye contact with the magistrate, who just nodded and changed the subject.

"From what Caterina has discovered with the help of Rafe Mathews, here," he said with a nod to the American, "was that Alice Perkins was the half-sister of Adrian Rook. From the text messages ostensibly between the two siblings, we believe that they planned to meet in Florence. Have I got that right, Caterina?" He held up the transcript of the cell phone texts.

Max was reading through his copy of the messages as Caterina summarized the communications between the two Americans for the benefit of Lt. Capra, Lt. Banfi and Marco.

"What I just learned on the way up in the elevator with Mr. Turner was that this appears to be the second death of Adrian Rook," said the magistrate with a wry smile. "If Antonio Bevilaqua is actually Mr. Rook, he apparently survived an American operation to exterminate him in Homs this past summer, only to die in Florence last night. So the true identity of the man in the Arno is our most pressing question next to, of course, who is the killer. I believe Caterina has some photographs taken by the coroner."

"So Max can identify the body in the morgue," said Marco. "Or perhaps, since he seems to have a 'need to know' my colleague, Lt. Banfi could also verify his identity."

Max shook his head. "I never met Rook. Rafe has."

"I, too, have never met Adrian Rook," said Franco Banfi. "I have some old surveillance photos in our files, but he is very careful not to be seen without a hat and sunglasses."

"Well, Caterina," said Rafe, his voice low and raw. "Let's see this man you folks pulled out of the river."

Caterina opened the file in front of her. She selected the head shots of the victim taken from various angles. She spread them in front of Rafe and pushed copies across the table to Lt. Banfi.

The room was completely silent. The magistrate and Max came to stand behind Rafe, who picked up one photograph and then a second and then a third. His face drained of all color. He cursed and said, "That's him. That's Adrian Rook. May he rot in hell."

"Are you sure?" asked Max.

"He's the reason I spent a month in a hole in Homs being starved and tortured. I would know him anywhere."

"But his face has been battered, probably by the river. It's not how he looked in life." Marco was looking over Lt. Banfi's shoulder.

"The only thing that could make it any clearer is if the coroner mentioned a tattoo on his left arm. It looks like a little castle with a crenelated pediment, but it is in three pieces – a forked top, a wide-footed base in the center, and a long rectangle at the bottom – but small." Rafe drew it on the back of one of the photographs. "See it's like a rook in the game of chess. A play on his name."

Caterina opened the folder again and drew out a photograph of the victim's left arm. The stark black tattoo on the pasty pale skin was identical to Rafe's drawing.

CHAPTER THIRTY-ONE

Max Turner whistled under his breath. "Adrian Rook, how did you make it out of Homs alive?"

Marco looked across the table at Rafe. "Mr. Mathews, it seems you have good reason to want this man dead. Where were you last night?"

"Marco!" Caterina pushed away from the table. "*Mio Dio*! Have you no shame?"

Rafe put a hand on her arm. "No, Caterina, he's right. I would have killed Rook in a heartbeat. But unfortunately someone beat me to him." He looked at Marco. "I was at my place in Piazza Tasso. Alone, sadly. No alibi witness." He paused. "But it seems that a little logic will tell you that I didn't kill Alice Perkins or Walid

Asfari although I probably don't have alibis for those deaths, either." He gave Max an exaggerated hangdog look. "My social life seems to be sadly lacking."

Max looked directly at Caterina, who blushed and sputtered, "Rafe is a friend of ours and needs no alibi."

Max turned to stare down Marco. "Rafe Mathews also has the full support of the U.S. government, which will not let his reputation and service to his country be tarnished by shoddy police work."

It was Marco's moment to backtrack, since his boss seemed happy to let him dangle. "I was just excluding him from our ongoing inquiry. I am working on a theory that Timo Monti is the fourth victim of this assassin and it all is tied to his uncle Leone Mollica's business shipping arms to extremists in Morocco and Egypt." He thought for a moment and then gave what Caterina assumed was his version of a hearty laugh. "Of course, Mr. Mathews you were at the Stibbert on that fateful evening. Again – wrong place, wrong time?"

Rafe's voice was icy, "I assume Timo Monti was the unfortunate young man in the knight's armor. I never learned his name. But if we are ready to get serious here, I may have some information that Italian authorities don't have that may be pertinent to the case at hand." He paused, then added, staring right at Marco, "It, however, has nothing to do with the killing at the Stibbert Museum."

Paolo Benigni moved back to his seat at the head of the table. "To what does this information pertain, Mr. Mathews?"

"Well, sir," said Rafe, turning his attention to the magistrate and modulating his tone as if to let off pent up anger. "Once I realized who the first victim found in the Arno was – that her name was Alice Perkins – I knew of her relationship to Adrian Rook." He paused and said to Lt. Banfi, "You may not know that Adrian Rook is the half-brother of Alice Perkins."

He opened the file that he had brought into the meeting. "When Caterina and Leo asked me to consult," he said, looking up at Lt. Capra, another dig at Marco, Caterina thought, "I wondered who the Australian fellow on the bridge really was." He then backed up a bit. "Of course, sir, that was before we knew Alice Perkins had been murdered with a blade and before Adrian Rook died. All we knew was that Alice was related to Adrian and that she was dead. I just wanted to complete the circle."

"What inquiry did you make?" asked the magistrate.

"I sent the photographs from Mr. Mundt's passport and mug shot to Langley and Interpol for facial recognition analysis."

Lt. Capra groaned. "Please don't tell me that I should have held on to him. What is he – an internationally known assassin?"

"I'm not sure you could have done anything different. Like Adrian Rook, Mr. Mundt had perfectly fabricated identification papers," Rafe said as he provided the magistrate and the threesome on the other side of the table with copies of the official NSA and Interpol documents.

The Interpol advisory contained a blurry photograph that looked like a still from a CCTV taken at an airport. The man in the photo was pulling a piece of luggage. He was identified as Dieter Mendel of Munich.

The NSA document had a passport photo and information regarding Damien Munier of Marseille, former member of the French Foreign Legion, freelance mercenary, and low-level arms smuggler.

"I see he kept his initials with each identity. That was smart," said Max. "So what do the folks at Langley and the NSA think he is up to?"

"The most convincing hypothesis is that Munier is his birth name and that after the kerfuffle in Homs, he decided that Adrian Rook's business was ripe for the taking."

"What about Walid Asfari?" asked Lt. Banfi.

"Although I just learned about his death today and haven't run this by analysts who are way smarter than I am, I do know the man by reputation. He was the hardliner in the Assad regime who was working to cut off the pipeline of arms, not only to ISIS, but also to the anti-Assad rebel forces. He would have been a roadblock to Munier's future business endeavors."

"So how do we find Damien Munier before he kills more visitors, either welcome or not, to our fair city," asked Paolo Benigni.

CHAPTER THIRTY-TWO

Within the hour, the search for Donald Mundt, aka Damien Munier, began in Italy and throughout the European Union. Max Turner returned to Rome. Marco Capponi and Lt. Banfi huddled with the members of the anti-terrorism division. Paolo Benigni went to check his mother out of the hospital, while Caterina and Rafe retreated to her apartment for a bowl of pasta and a bottle of Vino Rosso di Pitigliano. He stayed the night.

Unfortunately, Caterina thought, her mother chose Friday morning to stop by at dawn to see why her only daughter hadn't responded to a text message the evening before. Rafe answered the door since Caterina was in the shower.

"Mr. Mathews, I am somewhat surprised to find you here this morning," observed Margaret Mary. "Doesn't my daughter have to be at work soon?" She passed in front of him, heading to the kitchen to deposit a plastic container of roasted carrots and turnips, which was her second excuse for stopping by.

"Um, I believe so, ma'am." Rafe closed the door, tucking his shirt into a pair of black jeans before turning around. He scanned the room for his shoes.

Margaret Mary put two wine glasses in the sink before pointing a perfectly polished nail at the loafer sticking out from under the couch. "I am glad her father went off to the market an hour ago. I will put on a pot of coffee. Perhaps she will not be late."

"We were in meetings late last evening," Rafe started to explain before the coffee bean grinder drowned him out. He winced.

She pressed ground coffee into the filter basket of the Moka pot before responding. "Oh, I heard you arrive. You know, don't you, that her father and I live just across the landing here?"

"I think she mentioned…" The sound of the hair drier from the bathroom told him that relief was soon to arrive.

"I just wanted to assure her that I would be available to work at the Florentine Craft Fair next weekend. I believe she is meeting with the planning committee tomorrow."

Rafe slipped on his loafers and took a seat at the dining table as the bathroom door opened.

When Caterina entered the room in a chenille robe, while sliding on a wide headband to restrain her curly hair, she heard her mother say, "I believe your socks are under that throw pillow on the floor over there."

Caterina picked up the pillow, tossed it on the couch and handed Rafe his socks with a wink. "Mother, to what do we owe the honor?"

"Catherine, are those the boots you wore to the Stibbert Museum?" Margaret Mary asked, before clarifying, "Over there by the door. I almost tripped on them. You know if you want to keep them in good shape you need to polish them, put in wood forms and then store them in the box they came in."

"They were wet when I got home," Caterina said, knowing that she should just agree that her mother was right, as always.

"So they have been sitting there for almost four days. I got them for you, at no little expense, from Sergio Rossi. You must care for the leather."

"Yes, Mother. Again, why are you here?"

"As I was telling Mr. Mathews…"

"His name is Rafe."

"Rafe, then." She gave him a small smile as she poured shots of espresso into three cappuccino cups and added steamed milk. "I was saying that I wanted you to assure Patricia Benvenuti and Principessa di Belgioioso that I can work at the fundraiser at the American Consulate."

"It's a week away. You could have called or texted."

"I did. You didn't respond."

"My point is," Caterina said in a measured tone, "that you did not have to rush to dress this morning to deliver the message."

"You father was up hours ago. It was no rush."

Caterina knew her mother rarely emerged before ten, so the fact that she was dressed and coiffed by seven showed how curious she was about her daughter's visitor. She had tried to warn Rafe not to talk on the stairs or the landing the evening before.

"I'll let Pat know, but now that she has Bea Forzoni on board, I think it's under control." She looked at the boots in her hand as she walked into the bedroom, wondering why they evoked some connection that eluded her. Something about the Stibbert case.

Margaret Mary sat beside Rafe at the table and took a small sip of her coffee. She looked up as Caterina came back into the room, and said, "See if you can find out if Beatrice's mother is still in town." She saw her daughter's questioning glance. "Remember? I told you she had not been seen much since her son's death last year. I heard from Luciana Montalvo-Ligozzi that Signora Forzoni has gone to a retreat in Umbria with the sisters of Santa Chiara near Assisi. Luciana said she had a complete nervous breakdown."

"I'm certainly not going to ask Bea about that. You will have to use your usual channels," Caterina said, then turned to Rafe. "You know my mother would make a great intelligence operative." Seeing his eyes widen, she caught her mother's attention, "Mother, since it seems you are going to stay, why don't we let poor Rafe escape?

Maybe you can toast some bread and find the *marmellata* in the fridge while I dress for work."

At the door, she murmured to Rafe, "I expect the magistrate will appreciate an update on that matter we were discussing. Why don't you come to the Questura about three."

Rafe slipped on his jacket without a word, raised a hand in farewell to Margaret Mary and gave Caterina's hand a squeeze before she closed the door behind him.

She went back into the bedroom, got dressed and came out carrying the Sergio Rossi boots and the box, which also contained a pair of wooden stays, another gift from her mother, of course. As she slipped them into each boot, she asked, "Mother, have you been to Gucci recently? Can you remember if there is a logo on the boots this season?"

"Gucci? Of course not! I can barely stand to look in the window. The brand has had no class for a decade. It appeals only to those with a one season attention span. Kind of like an expensive Zara."

Caterina laughed. "It's not as bad as that." She closed the box and carried it back to her bedroom closet.

The aroma of toasted bread and fig marmalade brought her back to the table. "Thank you." She took a couple of bites. "So now that you have satisfied your curiosity, can I finish getting ready for work?"

"Hardly curious. I knew which way the wind was blowing ever since your father mentioned that you kept bringing Rafe to the family table at the osteria."

"Don't get your hopes up, you two. Rafe is most likely to head off to some dark dangerous place never to be seen again."

"I have more faith than you, it seems."

"Why is that?"

"No man whose mother named him William Raffaello grew up without being imbued with honor and good manners."

For once, Caterina had no answer.

CHAPTER THIRTY-THREE

Beatrice's brother died while racing in the multi-laned ring-road around the Fortezza da Basso. Ippolito Forzoni, known as Poli to his friends in the senior class at the private *Sacra Familia* high school, was piloting his Vespa GTS300. The powerful scooter was fast and nimble – witnesses reported seeing it weaving in and out of four lanes of heavy traffic – but it did not provide any protection for Poli when he went flying over the hood of an SUV that cut him off on the curve, while making a legal lane change. Too much testosterone, not enough sense, Caterina thought as she put down the report Patricia had left on her desk.

"Come in," she called in response to the knock on her office door.

Marco entered, already speaking before he sat down, "Another dead end."

"What is?" Caterina asked, pushing back from her desk.

"Timo Monti was not picking up missile launchers and grenades at the armory near Fiumicino. He was meeting his girlfriend, the daughter of the military base commander. She would ride south to the Naples port with him and then he would drop her off at the base on his way back to Florence."

"What was his uncle shipping to Egypt and Morocco in the crates that came north full of handbags and jackets to sell in the market stalls?"

"All legal, it seems," Marco said, shaking his head with disappointment. "I am still checking on whether he was reporting the taxable income, but apparently he has a deal with an electronics company in Pisa to ship components to factories that assemble small household appliances in North Africa, using his empty shipping crates."

"Sounds pretty wholesome."

"Lt. Banfi and the anti-terrorism squad are closing the file on Leone Mollica. The Stibbert case is being left to Captain Gentile. I guess his theory that this was a falling out between thieves is the right course of inquiry."

"But Timo Monti doesn't have any record of being a thief."

"There was that case when he was a kid and he certainly knew a bunch of miscreants among the players in the *Calcio Storico* teams." Marco stood up. "The magistrate agrees. It is not our case, but solely a local matter. No foreigners involved. Nothing for our task force to follow."

"I guess so," Caterina said, not mentioning that she had just determined that Timo Monti and Poli Forzoni were schoolmates at *Istituto Scolastico Sacra Famiglia*. As Marco said, it wasn't a task force case since no foreigners were involved in Timo's murder.

After Marco left, Caterina went back to the report of Poli's road accident. The driver of the SUV was a lawyer who had just picked her son up from pre-school. She and the boy were unhurt and she was not cited. The file was unusually complete for a road accident. Probably because Poli Forzoni's father was well-known in city business and political circles, Caterina thought. The list of witnesses and those who had stopped to help after the accident went on for pages. Despite his reported excessive speed, the case report contained no official determination of the accident's cause.

Caterina put the file in her outbox to return to Patricia. She thought about the different ways that the police force handled the cases of the two deaths of the school mates. Of course, they wouldn't have been friends, she thought. One was the descendant of Venetian nobility with a great future handed to him on a plate, the other the nephew of a tradesman, barely employable, who hung out with thuggish footballers. But both were dead; one deemed a thief and the other a tragedy.

She picked up the file again and walked it out to the administrative assistant's desk. "Thanks for the report, Pat.

It must have been a horrible time for Beatrice's family when the favorite son died so suddenly and senselessly."

"I can't imagine how his parents managed their grief," Patricia agreed. "In fact, I heard from one of the women working on the Craft Fair, who heard from Principessa di Belgioioso that Matilde Forzoni has gone to stay with her family in the Veneto. They own one of the Palladian villas in the countryside along the Brenta River. She's been gone for over three months. There's a rumor that she had a full nervous breakdown."

"My mother just told me this morning that Contessa Montalvo-Ligozzi told her that Signora Forzoni had joined the Santa Chiara convent near Assisi," Caterina said, shaking her head. "The ladies-who-lunch are definitely working overtime on this story."

Patricia nodded. "A lot of 'there but for the grace of God' goes into those conversations."

Caterina thought for a moment, then asked, "I know it's not our case, but could you do another thing for me, Pat?"

"Of course, my dear," Patricia said as she continued to sort the photographs and reports of the Walid Asfari murder into neat file folders and then, insert them into a three-ring binder. She looked up at Caterina's continued silence.

"It's probably nothing. But I noticed that Timo Monti, the man who was stabbed at the Museo Stibbert, attended *Sacra Famiglia* for two years. It would have been at the same time Ippolito Forzoni was there. I believe you talked to someone in the Records Office there. Could you find out if they were friends?"

"I can try to find out, but I would hardly think that they were pals, Caterina," said Patricia as she pulled a pencil out of the bun of hair on the back of her head. "They were in completely different social circles. I can't imagine Ippolito's father would have countenanced such a friendship."

"It's just something I want to clear up for myself. I remember something you said about Timo almost not graduating because of some incident."

"I can't remember what it was, but I'll call them again." Patricia handed Caterina the binder. "The magistrate asked that you have Rafe Mathews review this case. Something about a French suspect, named Damien Munier. The magistrate wants you and Marco to track the progress on the Asfari case and the ones involving the American siblings. You know, the deaths in the Arno."

"I will," she said, taking the documents. "I hope the resolution of the case will give Rafe some peace."

Patricia picked up another file. "You also have a new case. A German woman who operates an import-export business in Florence and Munich has brought a claim of fraud against a shoe company operating in Prato. The company's workers are almost entirely Chinese, paid subsistence wages, but the products are legally labeled 'Made In Italy' under the 2009 law. It seems you are going to learn about a whole new set of laws."

"But is this a criminal case?" asked Caterina. "Is it a police matter?"

"I guess that is what the magistrate wants you to figure out. It may be a case of criminals using immigrant labor. Or it may be as the woman claims a criminal fraud.

Or it may be something else. You are the perfect person to undertake the investigation. The magistrate suggests that you contact *Ispettore* Maria Teresa Serafini of *La Guardia di Finanza*, the Financial Police, who is charged with investigating the Chinese sweat shops in Tuscany.

CHAPTER THIRTY-FOUR

If Caterina hadn't known better, she would have thought Rafe actually looked bashful as he stood in her office doorway. Even though it was only five o'clock and the rain had stopped, it was dark outside her small office window. She hated it when the clocks were turned back each fall.

"I hope you didn't get too much grief from Margaret Mary," he said. "I meant to leave earlier, but you know…" His voice trailed off, but there was a suggestive gleam in his eyes.

"No hour would have been early enough to miss a visit from my mother," Caterina said. "She was up before dawn with my father and just waited until he left. She dressed and pounced." She grinned at him. "As for grief, she's delighted. My father, on the other hand…" She left it unsaid and his smile faded.

As she saw Marco coming down the hall behind Rafe's tall frame, Caterina changed the subject, "Let's take this out to the conference room, shall we?" She gathered up the three binders on her desk.

Marco started the meeting by describing his efforts to track the man using the identities Donald Mundt, Dieter Mendel and Damien Monier throughout Italy, employing the resources of the Carbinieri, the anti-terrorism division, and Italy's military intelligence.

"Evidence of his being in Italy, using any of the identities, shows he was hardly ever here. He was usually passing through on his way to Libya or Jordan." Marco passed copies of airline manifests to Rafe.

Rafe nodded. "He was probably just testing the waters; setting up preliminary contacts; wanting to see how the competition operated; and getting ready for any changes in business relationships. Arms trading, especially at the middleman level, is a high turn-over business."

"So you think he took advantage of the apparent opening left when Adrian Rook was targeted by U.S. Special Forces, during the operation to extract you from Homs?" asked Caterina.

"Probably," Rafe said, rubbing the area between his eyebrows. "Or he was planning to take Rook out himself and Jake's team gave him a gift, or so Monier thought." He opened the Asfari binder. "It may have been through Asfari that he learned that Rook was still alive."

"But how did he learn about the relationship between Rook and Alice Perkins? Or know that she was coming to Florence to meet her half-brother?" Marco asked.

"Maybe it was all Monier," said Rafe. "I've been thinking about this." He pointed at the other two binders. "Adrian and Alice weren't that close, but they certainly would have agreed to see each other, especially overseas. Rook couldn't get through U.S. immigration. He was black-listed."

"Are you saying it was all Monier pulling the strings?" asked Caterina.

"It's the only way it works, isn't it? Monier researches Rook's background and finds Alice. He sends her a phone and a ticket, pretending to be Adrian. It's the only way I can see that he would know where she was and how to get Rook to turn up."

"You're right. Rook must have been on hyper alert after the raid in Homs."

"So he gets Rook's contact information through Asfari or someone connected to Asfari," Marco chimed in, getting excited that there still may be something for him to take to the anti-terrorism division.

Caterina added, "He contacts Adrian via text, pretending to be Alice Perkins – 'Ciao, coming to Europe and going to be in Florence' – and he contacts Alice – 'Let's meet on the bridge' – he gets her drunk, uses her phone to contact Adrian one last time, stabs her and pushes her into the Arno."

"Then he meets Rook, kills him and thinking that in the turbulence of the *acqua alta* the Arno will carry the body all the way to Pisa or the sea." Marco paused. "So where is Damian Monier, now?"

"My guess is Syria or Libya," said Rafe. "The plan and execution were so precise. He had to have his exit planned."

Caterina interrupted him, saying, "Precise is not a word I would use. He got picked up on the bridge by Leo Capra's patrol officers. He got fingerprinted and his mug shot was taken."

Rafe laughed. "Everybody has an off day. But he kept his cool and handled you and Leo pretty well."

Marco smirked, but said nothing.

"So you are saying that he's not going to risk hanging around Italy."

"I expect that he got some of what he wanted with the deaths of Asfari and Rook, but he won't be taking over the business between the Calabrian mob and ISIS any time soon."

"Is that the only silver lining we are going to get?"

"And thanks to you and Lt. Capra, Interpol and the U.S. Intelligence services and their Italian counterparts now have a lot more to go on when trying to figure out who to look for and who may be trying to fill the void left by Adrian Rook." Rafe paused and added, "And in a twisted sort of way, I'm glad you didn't foil his plan to eliminate Rook. It saved me the trouble."

Caterina gave him a sidewise glance, not sure if he was joking.

Marco appeared to know. He offered a manly high-five to Rafe.

CHAPTER THIRTY-FIVE

Rafe and Marco, having bonded in male solidarity and bloodlust, went off to the corner coffee bar after Caterina told Rafe that she had about an hour of work left to do before her weekend began. Rafe promised to tell Marco how to write the perfect application to the FBI's National Academy.

As Marco told Caterina, "It's a professional course of study for American and international law enforcement managers nominated by their agency heads because of demonstrated leadership qualities. I believe that will not be a problem for me."

Caterina reserved judgment, but when he said, "The ten-week program—which provides coursework in intelligence theory, terrorism and terrorist mindsets, management, science, law, behavioral science, law enforcement communication, and forensic science…" all she could focus on was that Marco would be gone for *ten* weeks!

She interrupted his flow, assuring him, "You definitely have to do this, Marco. I think a reference from Max Turner, as the FBI's Legal Attaché in Rome, should be of great help. And Rafe will put that together for you, won't you Rafe?"

Rafe laughed and played along, putting the briefing binders in his leather satchel, "Let's go get a beer, Marco."

"It's a bit early for a beer, but maybe a spritz," was the last Caterina heard as she headed to Patricia's desk outside the magistrate's office.

"Patricia, I was just listening to Rafe and Marco talk about tracking cell phone calls and it got me thinking," Caterina started.

"About what, dear?" Patricia looked up, but continued typing on her computer's keyboard without slowing the pace.

"Did the police find Timo Monti's cell phone?"

"I believe so. I can check with Captain Gentile's assistant. Wasn't it mentioned in the briefing you attended on Wednesday?"

"I can't remember. I was wondering how he got into the cantina of the villa, where the costume that he was found in was stored. He must have been in contact with someone at the Stibbert before Monday's party."

"Maybe Marco has Mr. Monti's cell phone records. I believe he was looking at the Telepass computer printout to track Leone Mollica's trucks. The cell phone records would also have locational information of where the boy was when he was on his cell phone."

Caterina caught Marco and Rafe at the elevator. Marco nodded in response to her inquiry.

"They are in my outbox for Signora Benvenuti to file."

"Can I take them?"

"Of course. I don't need them anymore, now that it is not our case to follow. But drop the rest of the files in my outbox at the Signora's desk."

The elevator opened and he followed Rafe in. Before the door shut, Caterina saw Rafe mime hanging himself behind Marco's back. She was still laughing when she carried the two-foot stack of paper and files from Marco's office to Patricia's desk.

"Haven't you asked Marco to call you by your first name, Pat?"

"He hasn't requested the familiarity, so I haven't raised the issue."

"But you call him Marco."

"It's the privilege of the elderly, you know. In some ways I like those Italian cultural norms. In Australia, he would already have given me a nickname fitting my lowly administrative position."

"I can't believe that. Even in Australia you would have intimidated someone like Marco." She hefted the stack of paper to her other arm. "Where do you want me to put these?"

"On the table in the corner," said Patricia. "I'll get to them when I can. I want to take advantage of the fact that the magistrate is in one of his endless meetings at the

Palazzo Vecchio to get his correspondence typed. Marco tends to ask for every piece of paper possible and then without sorting anything, sends it back my way when he loses interest."

"I would think most of it could be shredded. Aren't these mostly duplicates of the official files?"

"Of course, but he's too busy with the important work to sort paper."

"Well, let me find Timo Monti's phone records and anything else from that case. If I can tell what should be pitched from the rest, I'll set it aside."

"Thank you, dear," Patricia said as she continued to type.

The files on the Museo Stibbert murder were about half way down the stack, but Caterina kept sorting. She pulled out a couple of reports on the Asfari assassination and left Patricia with two equal stacks, one to file and one to send to the document shredder in the bowels of the Questura.

She added the phone records to the rest of her notes on the Stibbert murder in her briefcase and stopped by Patricia's desk on her way home.

"I'll see you at your place tomorrow around noon. Is that okay?"

"Yes, dear. That will give you time to meet the others. Lunch will be served at one. It's a working lunch, but I think the last organizational bits and pieces will require most of the afternoon."

"Is there anything I can bring?"

"Just any good ideas. I wish the magistrate's mother could join us, but I hate to ask so soon after her procedure."

Caterina put her briefcase on the small couch in the reception area so that she could put on her rain coat. "Is she on the committee? You never mentioned her."

"Marcella was one of the founding members of the fundraiser years ago. She and Principessa di Belgioioso were the ones who thought that getting the foreign consulates involved would bring in the expats and right kind of tourists to highlight Florentine craftsmanship to a wider audience."

Caterina smiled, asking, "Who are the 'right kind' of tourists?"

"Why, the ones with money, of course! It is a fundraiser, after all. Art and cultural programs for the young in this day of social media and nonstop cell phone use is an imperative. More so now than when Marcella and the Principessa started the effort fifteen years ago."

"Have you asked the magistrate how his mother is doing?"

"I haven't wanted to bother him. He left at mid-day grumbling about these meetings, saying that he needed to spend more time at home."

Caterina picked up her briefcase. "I am sure with Bea Forzoni's organizational skills and with the advice of the rest of the committee, you will do Marcella Fontana-Benigni proud."

CHAPTER THIRTY-SIX

Concentrating on the task of pulling the cork out of a bottle of Brunello di Montalcino, Caterina missed what Rafe said.

"What was that?" she asked as she decanted the rich ruby wine into a wide-based blown glass carafe.

Rafe, lounging on the butter yellow leather couch, repeated, "Marco is going to have to learn to drink beer if he wants to survive ten weeks at Quantico. He ordered this orangey fizzing drink this afternoon. Never going to fly with the FBI."

She walked around the island counter that separated the kitchen from the living room and set the carafe in the center of her small dining table. "That was a spritz –

Prosecco, Aperol and a splash of soda. It's the only acceptable drink for an Italian before seven in the evening when we might order a Negroni, but only if appetizers are served."

"Like I said, he needs to graduate to beer if he doesn't want to stand out at the National Academy. Even the women drink beer."

Caterina ignored the last bit, commenting, "I don't think Marco minds being seen as special."

"Well there is special, and then there is *special*," Rafe said, patting the empty space beside him on the couch. He put the Asfari binder he had been perusing on the coffee table.

"Let me get some Prosecco if you don't mind a girly *aperitivo* before dinner." Caterina went to the refrigerator and pulled out a bottle of sparkling wine. She twisted off the thick cork and carried it with two slender glasses to where Rafe sat.

"I can't believe that Marco and Banfi missed the connection between Rook and Asfari. Just going through their files, it's clear why Damien Monier had to eliminate the Syrian."

"Will it help you find Monier?" She poured him a glass of wine.

"Perhaps. It gives us some of the rival contacts within Assad's circle to track the communication channels." He took the glass and waited for her to fill her own. "What was that toast I learned at the guys' party on Monday, something like 'Chianti' or '*cinghiale*' or..."

She tapped her glass against his. "I think you are thinking of *cent' anni*. It means 'one hundred years' that can either mean one hundred years of health or one hundred years of happiness."

He took a sip and waited until she took one, too. "I like the idea of one hundred years of happiness," he said as he leaned forward to kiss her, long and slow.

"Actually, *chinghiale* is what we are having for dinner," she said as their lips parted, before she mentally kicked herself for being such a doofus in the romance department.

He looked like he was about to make the same observation as he quirked an eyebrow, but he merely said, "Is that the famed wild boar I've heard so much about?"

She stood, took a long drink of the sparkling wine, filled her glass to the brim and retreated to the kitchen. "I'm making a spicy pasta sauce with ground boar. It goes with a wide noodle that one of Lorenzo's cooks makes by hand." She took the lid off a big cast iron pot on the stove and stirred the concoction inside. "I use Lorenzo's recipe, but I cut out half of the garlic he uses and add more chili pepper flakes and extra red wine."

"Is there anything I can do?"

"Just get some of my good wine glasses – the big ones – out of the *armadio* next to the table." She pointed at the carved wood cabinet against the wall. "The wine needs about thirty minutes, at least, to breathe and by then the pasta water will have boiled and the pasta will almost be done." She threw a handful of coarse salt into the simmering water. "Will *cavolo nero*, um, Tuscan kale, lightly sautéed, do for you? Or do you want a salad."

"I'm not a big greens person, so the kale's enough."
He put the long-stemmed wide-bowled wine glasses on
the table and retreated to the couch.

Caterina threw the *pappardelle* noodles into the now
boiling water, gave them a stir, set a timer for four
minutes, and went to join Rafe, pouring each of them
another glass of Prosecco. She kissed him this time
before taking a seat sidewise at the end of the couch, her
legs pulled up, bare feet near his thigh. He sipped his wine
resting a warm hand on her toes.

Unable to prolong the moment, she reached down to
a sheaf of loose papers on the floor. "Before you got
here, I was going through these phone records and I
wanted to ask you about what you remember of the
moments after we came across Katia next to Timo
Monti's body. It seems from the calls on his cell phone
that in the days before the party, he was talking to one or
two of the people working that night at the museum."

"Do you think you have identified his accomplice?"

She held out one sheet. "I don't know, but look at
who he was calling." She stood. "I have to check the
pappardelle." She picked up a slim file folder. "And look at
this. It explains why Timo was almost kicked out of
school right before graduation. I'll translate it for you, but
Patricia has already made a few notes in English in the
margins."

They discussed the wedding party, scavenger hunt,
layout of the museum, and the resulting discovery of
Timo Monti's body in the Hall of the Cavalcade as they
sipped Brunello and savored the wide ribbons of pasta
coated with a spicy thick sauce of wild boar. Slices of flat

ciabatta bread were used to clean the sides of the wide low pasta bowls.

"You might even get me to like vegetables," Rafe said. "I guess the trick is to cook them up with a lot of olive oil, hot peppers and garlic."

"That's what I always thought," said Caterina with a grin. "And not to overcook them. My father always claims that Americans hate vegetables because they cooked all of the flavor out of them."

"He may have a point."

Caterina cleared their plates off the table onto the nearby kitchen counter. "How about a little chocolate and maybe *biscotti*?"

"Do you have any of that *vin santo* for dipping. I had lunch with Leo Capra yesterday and he told me about that."

"Told you or showed you?" Caterina went to the refrigerator and searched back into a rear corner. She emerged with a tall narrow bottle. "I can imagine Leo tossing back a couple of glasses after lunch." She brought the sweet wine to the table with two shot glasses and a plate of *biscotti* and dark chocolate chunks. "It's one of my favorite desserts, too. The *vin santo* is made from certain specific varietals of white grapes that are dried before pressing and aged for a long time in small oak barrels. It's a perfect combo with *biscotti*."

"Leo told me to dunk the end of the cookie, count to five and then eat it." Rafe suited his words to the action of dipping the dry twice-baked almond cookie into the shot glass of wine and then held it up for Caterina to take the first bite.

"Perfectly done," she complimented him, savoring the now soft sweet wine-soaked crumbling cookie.

He dipped again and finished off the first *biscotto*. "Before we move on to more interesting things," he said with a suggestive wink. "I think you should call your boss about your suspicions."

"Now?"

"Now."

She stood and retrieved her cell phone from her purse and selected a contact.

"Sir, sorry to bother you at this hour. How is your mother feeling?"

CHAPTER THIRTY-SEVEN

Susan Whitmore, Consul General assigned to the U.S. Consulate in Florence, opened the wide double doors to Patricia Benvenuti's villa Saturday morning in response to Caterina's use of the whimsical brass door knocker in the shape of a dog's head with a bone between its teeth.

The two women kissed in greeting in the Italian style before Susan escorted Caterina through the foyer and living room, both festooned with ancient artworks and antique furniture upholstered with Florentine silk. In the fireplace, with its ornate Carrera marble mantle and pilasters, a lively fire of olive wood burned.

They entered the formal dining room where a long inlaid wood table, surrounded by tapestry-lined walls, was set with ceramic plateware with the Medici design picked out in yellow and blue and glassware from the Tuscan factory in Colle Val D'Elsa. A man wearing a white uniform jacket and black pants was putting the last touches on the centerpiece of colorful miniature gourds and dried artichoke flowers.

"Alessio, how are you?" asked Caterina. "And Violetta?" Alessio and his wife had worked at the villa for longer than Patricia had been married to Pietro Benvenuti. The young Australian had been welcomed and mentored by her older husband's houseman and cook until they became her extended family. After her husband's death they insisted they never planned to retire, but would remain on the estate for the rest of their lives.

Caterina knew that Patricia never needed the job with Paolo Benigni at the Questura, but when his mother suggested that her son could use the help setting up *la Task Force per gli strainieri* (Task Force for foreigners) serving expats and tourists living and visiting Florence, she readily agreed.

"We are doing quite well, Signorina Caterina," Alessio responded. "Ask Violetta to show you her new *filmino* of our grandson. He started school at the *asilo* in Fiesole last month. The Signora gave Violetta an iPad so we can see him on Instagram."

"What a big boy he must be," said Caterina, amused that the proud grandparents were getting a play by play of their grandson who lived less than thirty minutes away. "What is he? Five? Six?"

"Five years in May," Alessio said as he went through the door into the kitchen.

"Patricia is in the study," said Susan Whitmore. "She wanted to talk to you in private before the rest of the group arrived. I think Paolo called her this morning."

"I hope she isn't angry that the magistrate and I may change the agenda a bit today."

"She's just concerned that the fundraiser isn't affected."

"We'll make sure it goes forward as planned."

Within the next half hour the rest of the elegantly dressed planning committee arrived and were seated around the table as Alessio served a cream of pumpkin soup and Patricia introduced regular members – eight women and one man (the Consul General of France) – to the new recruits – Beatrice Forzoni and Caterina Falcone.

Behind Bea's chair at the head of the table was a large 18th century carved wood *armadio*. The top half was half of the depth of the base, which Bea used to prop a series of white display boards with plans for the Fair set out as talking points. She got up after the soup course and put up a list of the vendors. Caterina thought how elegant Bea looked in an emerald wool tunic over long soft leather boots.

"I've asked Carla, here, to help Beatrice with the organization of the vendors," Patricia said, nodding to a young woman with a short cap of russet hair that curled around her pale face. "Did you get a copy of the paperwork this morning, dear?"

Carla nodded, "Bea sent me an email with the vendor list and copies of all of the contracts attached, as well as all of the contact information. I only need a map of the layout for the booths in the Consulate."

Principessa di Belgioioso spoke up, "I know it is not raining today, *grazie a Dio*, but what will we do with so many vendors if we can't use the courtyard at the Consulate."

Susan Whitmore answered, "Our Consulate is prepared to make sufficient space available for everyone inside, except for the vendor roasting chestnuts and the young gentleman who is bringing his goats."

"Goats!" exclaimed the Principessa. "I didn't see them on the list."

Patricia spoke up, "Remember, Emiliana? The young man with the lovely golden curls who raises goats near Panzano. He makes cheese products and butter, as well as soap and lotion with goat's milk. He was part of the Fair last year and a big hit with the children. They are pygmy or miniature goats. Small and cute."

"We will provide a tent for the chestnuts and one for the goats," said Bea. "But let us all pray for a sunny weekend."

The conversation became general as small plates of *pasta con le briciole di pane*, thick spaghetti dressed with garlicky breadcrumbs, olive oil, and parmesan cheese, was served. This was followed by a discussion of the number and types of volunteers that would be needed. Hubert Lacroix, the French Consul General, agreed to help organize the volunteers.

"Dame Annabelle Berkshire, the new honorary Consul for Britain, couldn't be here today," said Susan, "but she asked to be assigned to a task, so I think she should assist you, Hubert, in the job of wrangling the volunteers."

"I can't understand why the British closed their Consulate in Florence," grumbled the Principessa.

"Budgetary reasons," intoned Patricia.

The Principessa snorted, "What is it they like to say? 'Penny wise, pound foolish.' That's it. Although Dame Annabelle is quite elegant…"

She was interrupted by Alessio's service of a light salad of autumn greens studded with chunks of poached salmon and slivers of red and yellow bell peppers. The sweet course was small individual apple tarts served with coffee. Alessio had just finished passing the cream when a knock sounded on the front door. He went to answer the door and escorted in Paolo Benigni, resplendent in turmeric-colored corduroy slacks and a tweed jacket, who had on his arm a petite older woman, wearing a vintage Chanel suit.

"Marcella!" exclaimed Principessa di Belgioioso, rushing around the table as fast as her bulk would allow to embrace her friend. "I had given up hope that you would join us. It didn't seem right to be planning the Florentine Craft Fair without you."

"Even my son couldn't keep me home, Emiliana dearest. Although he did try and then, insisted that he must accompany me when there certainly was no need." She kissed each of her friends around the table before saying, "He also insists that I can only stay for an hour. But let us see about that."

She turned to Caterina, who had been standing since the two entered the room. "You must be Margaret Mary's daughter. You have the look of your mother and certainly her stature."

Caterina blushed as she stood looking down at the elegant woman. "Signora Fontana-Benigni, it is a pleasure to finally meet you. My mother has mentioned your great friendship many times … and your son …" She hesitated to praise her boss in his presence.

His mother saved her from further speech and embarrassed her further by saying, "Paolo, of course, has told me of the fine work done by his newest recruit." She then turned to Beatrice Forzoni.

"Signorina Forzoni, I also know your mother. My thoughts and prayers are with her in this difficult time. Last year was definitely *annus horribilis* for your family," she said taking Bea's hand.

"Thank you, Signora," said Bea. "I am so glad you can join us. Your insights and those of the Principessa are so important to maintain the historical consistency for the Fair."

"That is a pretty compliment," said Marcella Fontana-Benigni, "but I saw what a strong woman you are with the production of the Maggio Musicale Opera Gala. Elegant, but modern. All of these annual events must change with the times."

She took Bea's chair at the head of the table. "It actually *was* my son who insisted that I come today. I believe that he and Caterina need your assistance with another matter, Beatrice."

CHAPTER THIRTY-EIGHT

Sun streamed through the glass garden doors into Patricia Benvenuti's study. After days of foreboding clouds and turbulent rain squalls, Caterina thought that the bright cloudless sky over the double rows of tall cypress trees guarding the wide path down the hill to the rear gate of the property and the bushy citrus trees in giant terracotta pots on the terrace was ironic given the conversation that was to come.

After she suggested that Beatrice make herself comfortable in a high wing-back chair, Caterina took a seat on the nearby wooden Savonarola stool so she could see the blonde woman's face. She put her cell phone and closed notebook with a pen on the small table between them. The magistrate lounged against Pietro Benvenuti's antique hand-painted writing desk.

"With what can I assist you?" asked Bea, as she crossed her legs and settled back into the chair. Her long finger traced the pattern of the jacquard silk upholstery.

"It was those boots, you know," Caterina started. "You were wearing those boots the first day I met you. Remember? I was with Rafe Mathews and Zandra Brooks. The meeting in the café at Museo Stibbert."

"I don't know what you mean. What do my boots have to do with anything?"

"It's just that Timo Monti didn't seem like the kind of guy who could afford to shop at Gucci. If he aspired to the brand, he surely would have acquired a knock-off from one of his uncle's Moroccan shipments."

"Timo Monti?" Bea's expression was perplexed. "Who is Timo Monti?"

"Remember the young man who died that night at the museum?" Caterina said, leaning forward.

"Of course, I remember him!" snapped Beatrice. "I'd hardly forget that horrible night. I thought it was Emilio Esposito, the boy I hired to wear the costume of armor. But he had left. I don't think I learned the poor man's name."

The first lie, thought Caterina. "Are you sure the police didn't mention Mr. Monti's name when they took your statement?"

"They questioned me that night. I don't think they knew who the victim was then."

Caterina feigned ignorance. "I'm sorry, I thought Lt. Lombardi came back to talk with you after the stolen items were found in Mr. Monti's car. Didn't he ask you whether they came from the Stibbert's collection?"

"I did talk with someone from the police after the theft was discovered, but I referred them to the museum's curator."

"And that same policeman told you that Timo Monti was the man who was murdered, correct?"

Bea looked at the magistrate and gave him a little half-smile, ignoring Caterina as she answered her questions. "I'm embarrassed to say, I didn't ask. I was just trying to put the whole tragedy behind me. You must know that in my business, reputation is everything. If one of my events was associated with a crime like a major theft at the venue and especially when that crime led to a death, my client list would evaporate."

Paolo Benigni made no comment. He looked at Caterina and nodded.

"Beatrice," said Caterina, waiting until the woman turned back in her direction. "Are you saying that you did not know the name Timo Monti until I mentioned it? You've never talked or texted with him?"

Bea's face became expressionless. "What are you saying? Of course, I didn't know him."

"The magistrate brought a warrant today," said Caterina, nodding to her boss. "It is for your cell phone. Would you please give it to him now?"

The magistrate drew an officially stamped and signed document from the inside pocket of his tweed coat. He handed it to Beatrice Forzoni and waited for her first to read it and then to take her iPhone out of the pocket of her tunic. He had her drop it into an evidence bag, which he sealed before returning to lean against the desk.

"My phone? My boots? What's going on?" Her tone was more angry than confused.

Caterina went back to her first statement. "I noticed your boots the first time we met. They are beautiful. The logo is so much more subtle than Gucci usually employs." She pointed at the interlocking golden G's on the outside ankle of each boot.

Bea hardly glanced down. "Again, to what purpose is your inquiry about my apparel?"

"Lt. Lombardi may have mentioned to you that the articles stolen from the museum were discovered in Timo Monti's car, but…"

"As I said, he did not mention the thief's name."

Caterina ignored the interruption. "But he may not have told you that the items were found in a Gucci shopping bag."

"So what?"

"The bag was a custom shape, not one of the standard bags for clothes. It wasn't until later when I was putting a pair of my own boots away that I noticed the size of the box. Long and narrow. Not the size that fits easily into a standard bag." Caterina felt she was getting tangled up in the minutia. The magistrate had agreed to let her take the lead on questioning Beatrice, but she knew he would step in if she was not getting the job done. For an hour that morning he had grilled her on every piece of evidence that she already had, every fact she needed to obtain, and how she should set up any further investigation needed to close the case. He then called

Captain Gentile and Magistrate Zaccheri to convince them that Caterina was the best person to conduct the interview.

She gave him a quick look. Benigni shook his head, making her push on. "The bag in the trunk of Timo Monti's car was a new shopping bag designed to contain boots, again not an item Timo would buy."

"Anyone can find a shopping bag. Why do you think it has anything to do with me?"

Caterina saw the magistrate glance down at the evidence bag on the desk, causing her to say, "Let me go to the second part of your earlier question."

"What question?"

"You asked why are we interested in your cell phone. Last week Timo Monti called your number twice. We have his telephone records."

"He may have called me, but I never talked to him or if I did, he didn't tell me his name. I talk to a lot of people when I am producing an event. You may have noticed the number of people working during the evening at the wedding reception."

"I was very impressed with the organization of the event and I noticed how involved you were in all aspects of the production."

Beatrice seemed to understand where Caterina was going with this line of questioning because she responded, "You would be surprised how much delegation is needed. Perhaps someone else involved in the planning gave this Mr. Monti my number. From what I gather, he was at the museum to steal from the collection. He had to get in somehow."

Caterina focused on her statement, "Exactly! Timo needed to be inside the museum undetected. Someone had to tell him how to get to the cantina and put on the suit of armor. Why do you think he would dress up just to steal the items found in his car?"

"To go undetected, as you say, I suppose. Maybe his confederate, the other criminal, the one who killed him, told him how to blend in. He certainly wouldn't have if anyone had seen his ugly face or his tattoos."

Caterina flashed back to when her boss told her that she should question Beatrice, saying, "You were there when the body was found and when Ms. Forzoni allegedly first saw the victim's face. You have all of the facts down cold and it is your hypothesis. Spin it out as long as you can to keep her talking. Perhaps you will be able to fill in the holes that still exist in the fact pattern."

Although she knew the answer Bea would give, Caterina asked, "When did you see Timo's face and tattoos?"

"When someone took the helmet off him. I was shocked. As I said, I thought Emilio was wearing that costume. The two men are much the same size, but Emilio is quite handsome."

Caterina sought to solidify what she thought would be Bea's next lie. "So you are telling us that you had never met Timo Monti before his body was discovered in the Hall of the Cavalcade."

"No, never."

"And you never knew who he was before today."

"Correct." Bea looked back and forth between Caterina and Paolo Benigni, as if trying to see the potential trap.

Caterina gave her a glimpse. "I believe your brother Ippolito knew Timo Monti."

Eyes wide, filling with tears, Bea whispered, "Poli? How can you say that?"

"Your brother Poli and you were quite close before his death."

The tears fell. "Of course. Are you inferring otherwise? Are you saying Poli would have anything to do with a thief? When he can't defend himself against the slander?"

Caterina tried to relax the painful tension in her shoulders as she slid farther back onto the carved wooden stool. "Timo was at school with Poli at *Sacra Familia*."

Bca's anger dried her tears. "Over one hundred boys attended that school. Timo Monti was a thug. My brother was a star. They would hardly run in the same circles."

"So you did know Timo." Caterina hoped this would catch her in a lie, but the hope was small.

"I could tell that from looking at his dead face. He was a thug and a thief. My brother was not friends with criminals."

"I didn't say they were friends, although there seems to be some evidence that they were." Before Bea could respond to this, Caterina changed course. "Your brother died in a traffic accent near the Fortezza da Basso, didn't he?"

Bea's eyes welled again. "Yes. It broke my heart and destroyed my mother."

"I am sorry for your loss and do not wish to dwell on that painful incident, but I need to know about what you believe happened in the accident. The police report said that Ippolito was driving his Vespa too fast and recklessly. He was hit by an SUV driven by a woman taking her child home from school."

"Yes, although it was total speculation that he was negligent. It was just a tragic accident."

"Witnesses said said he was weaving in and out of traffic."

"Maybe."

"Did you know that Timo Monti was one of the people who stopped at the accident scene to help your brother?"

Beatrice Forzoni sat statue-still, not appearing to draw a breath, her mouth open, her eyes staring somewhere over Caterina's shoulder. This went on for what seemed like minutes to Caterina. She didn't break the silence. It was probably only seconds, though before the magistrate straightened and moved into Bea's line of sight. She shook her head and pushed herself out of her chair to stand over Caterina.

"What are you implying?" she demanded.

Caterina paused before reaching to pick up the file she had left on the brocade-covered settee to the right of her seat. She flipped through the pages of the accident report to a list of all of the witnesses who were at the accident scene when the police and ambulance arrived. She showed Bea the list with Timo's name highlighted. "There was nothing more than his name; no statement attributed to him, but he appears in one of the photographs of the accident scene, part of the crowd. It was taken after Poli was placed in the ambulance."

Beatrice turned abruptly away. "I certainly do not care to see it. Are you so heartless?" She paced toward the magistrate and then seemed to notice him in her way and returned to her chair. She sat down, running a weary hand through her hair. "I did not know that he was there."

"But you learned about it later," Caterina said, closing the file.

"I mean I did not know that he stopped."

Caterina rephrased her statement, "You learned later that Timo Monti was racing with your brother from the Cascine Park by the Arno, around the Fortezza, and back to the park." Caterina knew that she was working from theory, not fact, but it was plausible. "Someone told you — maybe at Ippolito's funeral, maybe after — that the boys at school were saying that Timo won the race by default because your brother didn't finish. He crashed."

Shaking her head in denial, Beatrice said nothing.

Caterina continued, "The school authorities heard of the boasts, not from Timo or his supporters, but from one of Poli's mates, who claimed to know that Timo had caused the accident. They suspended Timo while this claim was investigated, but it came to nothing. None of the witnesses to the accident had seen another Vespa near the crash."

Bea seemed to decide on her path. "I can't remember. That time was all a blur for my family."

"I think you do remember. I think you mourned the loss of your brother, and then endured the painful decline of your mother into depression. You found you couldn't

take Ippolito's place with your father." Caterina saw out
of the corner of her eye that the magistrate was moving
in her direction. She knew she was putting too many
words in Bea's mouth and should be asking questions, not
making statements. Before his hand came down on her
shoulder, she said, "Your anger against Timo Monti grew
unabated. Your brother was dead and you thought Timo
should be, too. You decided to take revenge."

Paolo Benigni lowered himself onto the settee,
waiting for Beatrice's response.

It came in anger. "You think I killed Timo Monti?
Absurd! He was a criminal and was killed by one of his
confederates."

Caterina leaned forward, speaking softly, almost
confidentially, "That just doesn't fit, Bea. Timo graduated
from *Sacra Famiglia*. He became a truck driver. He had a
girlfriend. He never got into trouble with the police – not
even a speeding ticket."

"But you saw him – the tattoos and the broken nose.
He was a thug."

"He was a team member of the Santo Spirito *Bianchi*
squad, competing in the *Calcio Storico*. It's a rough game,
and even though I am the first to admit many of his
teammates are petty criminals, there is no evidence that
Timo ever engaged in any wrongdoing. He was living his
best life."

"But he stole from the museum. The items were
found in his car." Bea locked eyes with Magistrate Benigni,
as if he would agree with the factual evidence even if his
inspector had another view of the victim's nature.

"That brings us back to the boots," said Caterina. "As I said, you decided Timo played a part in your brother's death and you decided to take revenge."

Bea changed tactics. "Revenge, me? How could I kill someone, much less someone as strong as that man?"

"You knew you needed to have him at a disadvantage. Constrained somehow. You thought of the armor. You contacted Timo and asked for a favor. Perhaps you even offered to pay him. He may have been surprised, but he knew you were Poli's sister. That's why I said earlier that I felt that Poli and Timo were actually friends. Early in Timo's school records there was some mention that he was a loner when he started school as the new kid, but that someone befriended him. When the school authorities investigated the claim of the cause of the accident, the race was described as between two friends. He probably thought of you as the sister of his friend, a friend he owed a debt through no fault of his own. He had no idea that you blamed him."

"I don't know why you are making up all of this speculative drivel. You haven't said a single factual thing. I never knew Timo Monti. I never met or talked to Timo Monti. I am going to get my father to stop these defamatory accusations."

Caterina went back to her confiding tone. "Your biggest mistake was the Gucci bag. The theft had to be done by someone with access to the keys to the cabinets in the museum the night of the party. That was either you or your helpers."

"Have you talked to each of them?"

Caterina refused to be drawn by Bea's misdirection. "You agreed to let Emilio Esposito leave early, as Emilio told Lt. Lombardi. You probably met Timo when he drove up in his car. He would not have known the neighborhood. You asked to put a bag in his car's trunk. Maybe you asked for a ride home later. You showed him where to park. Not too close."

"Magistrate, I insist you stop participating in these lies," Beatrice stretched a hand out to him.

He stood and went back to the desk as if to create some distance, to remove any imagined support. "Finish it, Caterina."

"You took Timo into the cantina and showed him the costume. You took him into the Hall of the Cavalcade during the toasts after dinner. You weren't seen at the party during that time. Photographs taken by the guests will back this up. Perhaps you told Timo to wait in the grand hall because the guests would be participating in some after-dinner activity. You knew that your helpers, who were closing up the museum, would get to that room last. You stabbed him, leaving him on the floor where he was found about thirty minutes later. In the meantime, you went to get the presentation of the cake underway."

"This is all an absurd lie." Beatrice crossed both her legs and her arms, armored against the story Caterina was spinning.

Caterina stood. "No, it is means, motive and opportunity. If your phone contains any evidence of contacts with Timo Monti and if after your fingerprints are taken, they match the two prints found on the Gucci shopping bag, and if your fingerprints are found on the suit of armor, I believe that the rest of the case will fall into place. My guess is that – now that we know what to look for – your DNA will be found, either on the suit of armor, or on the knife, or on Timo, or in all three places. It is hard to stab someone and not leave a trace behind."

"I want to see my father. I want to talk to a lawyer."

Caterina felt the adrenalin leave her system. She stood and walked toward the door as the magistrate took over.

"Beatrice Forzoni, you will be arrested today and taken by Lt. Lombardi and another officer, who are presently on the premises, to the *Commissariato di Pubblica Sicurezza*, the police station, in Montughi, where the crime took place. You will be allowed to make your telephone calls once the preliminary custodial steps are completed."

"You will not get away with this travesty," Beatrice snarled. "It is only your word against mine what happened here today. My father will never allow the family name to be tarnished by the words of an incompetent girl playing at being a police inspector."

"Well it is lucky that you will have a complete transcript of our conversation today for your lawyer to work with," said Caterina. "I almost forgot I left this here." She walked back to the small table by Beatrice's chair and retrieved her cell phone. "I will make sure you get a copy forthwith." She turned the Voice Memo function off.

Later, after Lt. Lombardi had escorted Beatrice away and the assembled committee participants had absorbed the idea that they would have to enlist more help for the

Florentine Craft Fair, Paolo Benigni prepared to escort his mother home. He pulled Caterina aside.

"Good work today, Caterina. However, once you file your report with Captain Gentile, you are released from all duties until a week from Monday. You are assigned to make sure this damn fundraiser is a success. My mother will never let me hear the end of this unless this Fair brings in significantly more this year, than last year."

Caterina laughed. "Then I suggest you pray that the rain has ended for the season. You know that the American Consulate sits on the bank of the Arno. Also, you might think of pulling out your check book. Patricia is the treasurer. I'm sure she would appreciate receiving your donation to such a worthy cause."

CHAPTER THIRTY-NINE

The Arno, clouded with silt and mud, still raced along its course at unusual speed, but as evening fell the sky was dotted with only a few golden rosy clouds, lit by the sun setting downriver. Across the waterway from where Caterina and Rafe sat at the lone table on a tiny café balcony, the lawn of the rowing club had reemerged, soggy, but still green.

"Despite the sinkhole on Lungarno Torigiani, it looks like the city has dodged the next big flood one more time," Caterina said after taking the first sip of her Negroni cocktail.

With a tiny pronged wooden pick, Rafe snagged an olive from the selection of snacks that came with their drinks. "As exciting as your father made the Great Flood of 1966 sound, I'm glad we are going to enjoy a few days of unseasonably warm weather before winter sets in." He swallowed the salty olive and drank from a large glass of craft beer from *Birrificio Del Ducato*. "This is good, but why can't they serve a regular draft like Peroni or Menabrea?"

Waving a hand at the nearby Ponte Vecchio, Caterina said, "Fancy beer goes with the view."

He nodded and took another swallow. "I assume that it's going to be dark, cold and damp for the next three months."

Caterina grinned. "You are mostly right. Although if we're lucky, we'll get an inch or two of snow. It will only last a day, maybe two, but there is nothing more magical than Brunelleschi's Dome powdered white and the streets lit by glittering holiday lights with flakes drifting down from above."

He changed the subject. "I'm so glad that you lucked out with a great weekend for the fundraiser at the Consulate, although it's going to take me awhile to forgive you for volunteering me for goat wrangling."

"I thought you did a great job herding the kids and … the kids." She chuckled at her own joke. "Get it?"

"Got it." He threw an almond at her, which she ducked, so it dropped into the river.

"Hey! I thought you were a ranch hand from Wyoming. It was clear that Teodoro needed help when the families descended on his tiny herd. At least you didn't have to demonstrate how to milk a goat."

"I'll have you know I grew up in the Rocky Mountains of Colorado. The only animals I ever cared for were our beagle Boswell and the mean gallery cat my mother kept among her art. I know more about craftsmen, than livestock. You should have put me inside with the ceramic artisans and fancy Florentine papermakers."

"Pretty refined experience for a spy." She pitted an olive before eating it.

"It takes all kinds, but now that you mentioned it, I need to tell you that I'm probably going to miss the holiday lights … and snow."

Caterina felt a sense of dread; fear that he was going back to some Middle East hellhole. She plucked the orange rind out of her drink and began to shred it into tinier and tinier pieces. The last couple of weeks had been the highlight of her year. Not only had the resolution of the Stibbert murder with the arrest of Beatrice Forzoni come largely from her own investigative work, but she and Rafe had grown closer, spending most of their free time together. He was even a regular at the Falcone family Sunday lunch table in her parents' apartment.

"Why?" was all she managed to say.

"Oh, no! Sorry!" he exclaimed when he saw the look on her face. "It's nothing dire. Langley just wants me back at a desk in D.C. to provide analytical support in the hunt for Damien Monier. I expect I'll be back in Florence by mid-January. They just want to drain my tiny mind of every last fact, conjecture, and idea regarding both Adrian Rook's old lines of communication and commerce and those that Monier may have put together."

"But you are going to miss my mother's Thanksgiving dinner. She specifically asked that I invite you. It is the *only* meal she cooks all year. She insists on the classic menu with turkey, stuffing, cranberries, and pumpkin pie. She makes sure the ingredients she can't get here come in someone's suitcase."

"Much as I fear disappointing Margaret Mary, we can't delay capturing Monier. If he's given that much time, he will likely be able to go to ground and avoid detection."

"But the Italian intelligence services are working on the same thing," she argued. "Can't you stay here and work with them or with Max at the Embassy in Rome?"

He shook his head. "The folks in Washington think I will be more efficiently used there. Frankly, I think that the Agency doesn't want to share some sources and methods with our Italian brethren." He reached across the table, swept up the orange peel bits, and tossed them into the river. He took her hand between his. "Hey, Sweet Pea, it's not going to be that long. And here's what I have been thinking about ... I bet you haven't had time off this past year. I thought all Italians headed for the beach or the mountains in August for four or five weeks. But you were chasing after that American woman." He paused. "What was her name?"

"Melissa Kincaid."

"Yeah, the Texan," he said, squeezing her hand tighter. "Why don't you take a couple of weeks and come stay with me? They are setting me up with a place in Alexandria. I'll have a rental car. I can show you the sights."

Caterina sat back. He let her go. A look of concern crossed his face.

The idea appealed to her. First, she smiled at him with great tenderness, but then the smile turned into a wicked grin.

"That's a wonderful idea, Rafe. You are so sweet to offer to play host. Maybe I can take an extra week and bring my mother. Did you know that all of Margaret Mary's family lives in and around Boston? She loves going to the East Coast for holiday shopping after Thanksgiving." She took one of his hands this time, and looked deep into his eyes, "How big did you say this 'place' in Alexandria is going to be?"

Rafe groaned until he realized she was joking. He kissed her hand before their joined laughter danced across the River Arno.

ACKNOWLEDGEMENTS

The Museo Stibbert is one of the most eclectic and fascinating museums in Florence, but it is rarely visited by tourists, at least not on their first trip to Florence. With its extensive gardens, it is the perfect place to beat the heat and escape the crowds during the Florentine summer. To my knowledge, however, there has never been a murder committed in the museum.

Many of the locations in this novel, including the Ponte Santa Trinita, with its interesting and potentially dangerous architectural features, actually exist and are worth a visit, but all of the events described herein are fictional.

The photographs on the front and back covers of the first edition of *Revenge by the Arno* were taken by Joe Messina of TCR World Photography. Although these are the first photographs taken by Joe that have graced one of the covers for the Caterina Falcone mystery series, he has been gracious in supplying me with photographs for this and the other books to sharpen my memories of Florence.

Jim and Barbara, again, had the unenviable task of first readers and I thank them. RoJean, Nancy, George, Monica, Christine, and Barbara (again) reviewed later drafts and I am grateful for all of their corrections and suggestions. Francesca checked my Italian usage and found it woefully lacking, but fixed the errors. All remaining overlooked errors of fact, fiction, spelling and punctuation are solely mine.

My father suggested that a murder mystery that harkened back to the 1966 flood when the Arno crested its banks and drown the city would be an interesting challenge. He was right and I thank him for the idea.

THE AUTHOR

Five years used to be Ann Reavis' attention span for any career. She's been a lawyer, a nurse, a presidential appointee in a federal agency, a tour guide and a freelance writer. She's lived in New Mexico, Texas, California (San Francisco Bay Area), Michigan and Washington, DC. Then she broke the pattern when she spent fifteen years in Florence, Italy, learning to be Italian. She published *Italian Food Rules* and *Italian Life Rules* to celebrate the experience. For now, she has settled back into life in Washington, DC, where she has turned her hand to mysteries and thrillers set in Florence and Tuscany.

35358212R00163

Made in the USA
Middletown, DE
09 February 2019